WARDEN

BLADE ASUNDER BOOK 3

PAPERBACK
FANTASY

WARDEN

JON KILN

CHAPTER 1

Queen Myriam was saddened. This should be one of the happier moments of her short life with her ascendancy to the throne, yet all she could do was grieve. She was only just coming to terms with the murder of her parents, King Ludwig and Queen Alissia, murdered by the usurper Duke Harald. She had been numbed to the events unfolding around her, but now, she had to face her losses. Her people were relying on her. Not too long ago she had been a happy princess, living out her life at Castle Villeroy, being trained and prepared for the moment when she would rule. Now, she was the Queen of that castle and all its lands. She had to make the decisions and lead the armies.

Luckily, she did not have to face these difficulties alone. She had a close and trusted entourage who would lay down their lives to keep her safe. Friends who had stood by her side in her darkest hour and helped her overcome the evil tyrant, her uncle. Not only had he beheaded her parents, he had proven to be a cruel man.

Her people were looking to her to help them move from the darkness of her uncle's rule, and into a brighter, better future.

The people might be joyous now, while they celebrate his death and their new Queen's crowning, but soon they would remember the changes he had enforced and the loved ones they had lost while ruled by his cruel hand. Higher taxes needed to be lowered again, and freedoms he had curtailed restored. The deaths of many during the battles needed to be mourned and losses recompensed. Indeed, she had much to undo that her Uncle Harald had inflicted in his short reign on the people who lived in the Kingdom of Palara.

As if the politics of such times were not enough to concern her, she also worried over the disappearance of her grandmother, the Duchess D'Anjue. Were it not for the Duchess's bravery, these lands may still be ruled by the cruel usurper.

In the short time she had spent with her grandmother, when she had taken her under her wing at Castle Locke, Myriam had learned what a strong and loving woman her mother's mother truly was. Despite her own loss at the death of her daughter, Myriam's mother, she still managed to ensure that her granddaughter had escaped the castle when the usurper's men came for her.

Myriam had already decided that she must find her grandmother. She knew that she was alive, as the magic of the stones of Berghein linked the D'Anjue bloodline, inexorably. Although the Duchess did not hold one of the stones, they would have told Myriam if her grandmother was gone from this world. Yet no path they followed had yet led to any indication of the Duchess's whereabouts. Also, the strange little monk Ghaffar, who had managed to release her grandmother from the dungeons, had disappeared aswell. There had to be a link.

Queen Myriam went out onto the large balcony of the castle. She had been instructed of her duty to show herself to the gathered people. Myriam knew her responsibilities, what was expected of her, but she did not seek their adulation. She only wanted to rule in their best interests. Her family had much to make up to them.

As she waved and smiled to the cheering crowds, she was not alone. By her side stood Artas, a nobleman who had also lost much. His parents, too, had been beheaded for their loyalty to the King, her father. Artas was her friend and guide and she would need his council over the coming days. His bravery in battle and loyalty to the royal family had earned him a knighthood. He like many brave soldiers and fighting subjects, were to be rewarded for saving their kingdom.

Myriam had asked Ganry, the former mercenary turned bodyguard, to lead her armies, but he had refused the role. Leading armies was too much a reminder of Ganry's former life, which ultimately led to pain and sorrow. He felt his talents were now best served at her side, as her personal protector.

This she could not refuse for she had come to rely on him and his strength. He wanted no riches, no lands, only to live in Castle Villeroy. Many call him a retired mercenary, but he would argue that his sword was still active, should anyone ever dare to threaten his Queen.

She had provided for him in the castle, giving him his own quarters and manservant to help, and he was now head of the honored Queen's Bodyguards. This role he was happy to take, knowing that only those who he had personally chosen could get close to her. The arrangement also suited Myriam. With the loss of her parents she was in need of many who could advise her, and Ganry was one of few who she truly trusted.

Looking out over the castle grounds and the village, she enjoyed all the adornments in an array of beautiful colors. The town had been decorated with hanging streamers of colorful banners and ribbons. The people wished to bring brightness and joy back into the Kingdom of Palara, and they hoped that with the crowning of a new Queen would come prosperous and more peaceful times.

Whenever their Queen looked out of her windows, she would feel uplifted and her grief would ease with the love of her people. King Ludwig had kept peace over the lands for many decades and his people had loved him for it. Now, they had the same hopes in his daughter.

Myriam wanted nothing more than to find peace for her people. Yet first she must find her grandmother, her only living relative. Surely the people would not deny her this small favor.

CHAPTER 2

In looking for a solution to find the Duchess, Myriam called a private meeting. She wanted only her most trusted advisors and friends. Being still uncertain of the loyalties of most of the politicians and noblemen, of which many had supported Harald in his reign of terror, she was wary of them.

A week ago she had contacted Hendon, the forest dweller. She would also liked to have Linz here too, but he was now chief of his tribe and had much work to do there after the ravages of battle.

There was a strange and unknown link in their bloodlines, previously undiscovered, between Myriam, Hendon and Linz, which they only became aware of as they all gained a skill from the Berghein stones. Only those of the D'Anjue bloodline were blessed with this. These stones also allowed them to visualize each other's surroundings, even when they were hundreds of miles away from each other. A basic means of communication, but nonetheless, it had proved a useful one.

Hendon had arrived the day before and now sat with the Queen and Ganry in the garden, enjoying a light meal while they awaited for the arrival of Artas. He could soon be seen arriving with a unit of soldiers who made their way towards the stables. Artas saluted to the Queen and Myriam waved him over, eager to get the meeting started.

Artas joined them at the table, and the discussion began in earnest.

Hendon was telling us about his new staff, Myriam said, for the benefit of the new arrival. Turning to Hendon she continued, "You say it has a spirit of the dead within?"

"Upon my return, I found the staff at my home in the forest, so I began to carve it to make it more personal to my needs. As I was finishing, the staff told me that it was glad I'd finally stopped hacking away at it. At first I did not know who spoke to me, in my mind. It wasn't until the staff floated in the air and knocked me on the head, that I realized it is alive. I've yet to work out who it is, but I suspect it is the soul of Barnarby of Bravewood. I do not think we have seen the last of him," Hendon told her.

"Oh, I do hope so, Hendon." The thought of Barnaby brought a tear to her eyes. He had hardly known her, yet had given his life to help her escape those wretched soldiers that her uncle had used to hunt her down. "He was an odd character and I would love to thank him for all the help he gave to my cause."

Myriam was pleased to learn that Hendon's special skills were improving. She had been aware that he could communicate with animals, but now he was able to communicate with the trees and the winds and all manner of things.

"You remember Barnaby, whom we thought a wizard?" Myriam said to Ganry, who looked on, skeptical, at Hendon's tale.

"I still maintain that there is no such thing as magic," Ganry retorted, knowing full well he had witnessed so many unexplained events during the coup.

"Yes, yes, we know how you feel Ganry, but Hendon believes that Barnaby has put his soul into this staff. Does that not convince you that there is indeed some elements of magic to the world?" Myriam said, determined that she would get Ganry to come to terms with what to her, was so very obvious.

"All it convinces me of, is that the young master Hendon is a little too familiar with the local hooch."

That brought a smile to everyone's lips, even Hendon's.

"Shall we take this meeting inside? It is after all meant to be a secret gathering," Ganry suggested.

"Only what we are discussing is secret," Myriam said. "If we hide away then suspicions will arise. I thought if I meet with my friends out in the open, no one will suspect a thing. Clever, don't you think?"

"Yes," Ganry said. "I am pleased to see you starting to think like a Queen at last."

Myriam gave him a look of annoyance, even though she knew his words to be true. It was difficult for her, adapting so quickly, but she knew she had to, and Ganry's advice was always given out of love and respect.

"Thank you Ganry," she smiled at him. "It is hard going from a mere princess to bossy Queen. Artas," she said, attempting to change the course of the subject, "update us on the search for the Duchess."

"No news, I'm afraid," Artas informed them. "My men have searched everywhere and questioned many, yet still the Duchess's whereabouts remain a mystery."

To any casual onlookers, the group would appear to be nothing more than a group of friends enjoying their reunion. No one could have guessed that they were discussing a quest for the Queen. And a dangerous one at that.

Though Ganry would have her stay at the castle, Myriam insisted that she go and find her grandmother. It was the least she could do for all the Duchess had done for her, including losing her castle and risking her life. Ganry could find no argument with this, even though he tried to convince her otherwise. She was as stubborn as always.

CHAPTER 3

Linz was suffering much the same treatment as Myriam. When his uncle had been killed by the lizard man, he had become Chief of his people, the Lake tribes. No amount of preparation was enough for the huge responsibility and the expectations of this role, even though he had been in training for most of his life.

There seemed to be a never ending amount of disputes amongst the people that he was expected to resolve. The list of tasks for the Chief was endless. He never realized that his uncle had so many responsibilities. The most difficult ones at the moment were the funerals and burials of the brave soldiers they had lost, in the recent battle of the coup at Castle Villeroy.

He had wanted to help Myriam gain back her rightful place on the throne, in the Kingdom of Palara. Historically, his people were always a part of the Kingdom, but his predecessors, including his uncle Chief Clay, had chosen to keep the Lake People hidden from the other races of this land.

Now they were discovered, but with the Queen's help, they could at long last have rights to the land they had chosen to settle in. They lived deep in the forest of Cefinon, where few from the kingdom ever ventured.

The city of Halawa, with its wooden houses on stilts, was now officially on the map. It was the new Chief's hopes that trade would bring a little more wealth to his people. Though Chief Linz is young for such responsibilities, he has good advisors, including hand picked ones sent by the Queen from Castle Villeroy.

He knew his friends were meeting with the Queen, but he had decided not to become involved in the search for the Duchess as he needed to be here for his people. Many had suffered losses in a battle that he had supported. Now, he believed, it would be wrong for him to desert them in this, no matter how much he wanted to go.

He had discussed this at length with his mother Lisl, who was his most valued and closest advisor. She argued that now would not be a good time to be absent, and he reluctantly agreed with her. His uncle had relied on his mother's wisdom in difficult and challenging times, and so would he.

He had moved into the Chief's hut, and his mother had moved in with him. He felt better being surrounded by those who he trusted and could rely upon. Good advisors would help and guide him as he tried to improve the lives of his subjects. They were a simple people, not needing the comforts of luxury, but he wanted to bring education to them and access to travel so they could better understand the world around them. A world, that, for most of them until recently, was a mystery.

Myriam had given him books to read and although his reading skills were basic, he was improving every day. Blowing out the candle as he finished reading of the Holy War, which had involved his ancestors in the D'Anjue bloodline, he sighed at the coming night.

Sleep had been hard to obtain with all his new worries, and many a night he would toss and turn while his mind was filled with the responsibilities of leadership. At fourteen years old he did not feel ready to take a wife, but he looked forward to the day when he could share his worries with someone he loved.

Before he could sleep, he thought of the monk, Ghaffar, who had lived in the temple on the lake. He wondered at his whereabouts, because he was the last one to be seen with the Duchess D'Anjue. His people watched the temple but and there were no signs of Ghaffar's return.

Setting his thoughts aside, he closed his eyes to invite sleep, and soon his world was relaxed and he slipped into a light slumber. But not for long. One of the reasons for his restless nights were the dreams, vivid and real.

Tonight he was stood on a battlefield, surrounded by the dead. Before him was a lizard man, readying his spear to strike him down. He noticed the beast held a human head in its claws. Its scaly fingers entwined with long brown hair. Was it one of his own tribe, as the males all have long hair? It was hard to tell as the hair fell in such a way to obscure the face. The lizard man raised his macabre trophy and the hair fell from the visage, revealing the features of the Duchess, eyes open and staring right at him, accusingly.

"No!" Chief Linz yelled out, suddenly sitting upright. He felt disoriented, but in a few moments he realized he had been dreaming again. Yet it did not feel like a dream. It felt so real that his body was soaked in sweat and the adrenaline coursed through his veins.

Getting up to take some air, he went out onto the wooden porch that surrounded his hut, beneath which was the lake. The water was rippling even though there was no breeze. Curious as to what was causing the water's movement, he went to the rail and peered into the murky depths. It took a while before his eyes adjusted but when they did, he saw that there were at least a hundred water lizards gathered around his hut.

Linz felt a cold shudder run through him. The water lizards had never behaved this way before. This could only be a foretelling of things to come. Desperate for an answer to this puzzle he ran straight to his mother's room, shaking her awake and telling her of his dream and the phenomenon in the lake.

"It is a message from the lizard people," she said, feeling an urgency. "They are calling you, Linz, they want to guide you to their home, but I know not why. My son, I do not think it will be safe. It is trickery, please don't go," his mother pleaded with him.

"I have to go see Myriam, mother, it is something to do with the Duchess and I must tell her. Do not forget, our ancestors are one and the same and we share their bloodline. We cannot turn our heads to our own."

"What will you do, my son? We have lost so many of our people to the Queen's cause, do we really want to go to battle so soon?"

His mother spoke wise words, but he could not turn his back on the Duchess. She had helped Myriam's cause and she was clearly in danger.

"Tomorrow, I will travel to see the forest dweller, Hendon. Together we can contact the Queen and I will tell her of my fears. Go to your bed, mother, you will stand in my stead whilst I am gone. I can't help but feel that our people are involved in the Duchess's life. I bid you a good night's sleep for what is remaining of the darkness. Soon I will pack and will be gone before you awaken."

She hugged her son. Always, she trusted his judgment, just as he trusted her wise words. He had been trained all his life by her brother, Chief Clay. He would make the right choices for his people.

CHAPTER 4

Linz took one other person with him as it is not wise to be alone in these forests, even though he had lived here all his life. All manner of dangers lurk in the shadows. If one is injured, then the other can seek help. If both are injured then all they can do is pray.

Wyatt was a brave warrior, tall and strong, and he seemed always to be stuck by Linz's side. He must have taken it upon himself to guard the new Chief, or his uncle had allocated him the chore before this death. Whatever the reason, Linz liked Wyatt and trusted him to accompany him on this mission.

Soon they were passing the large summer house that belonged to the Stapleton family, on the edge of forest Cefinon, but this time he did approach it. When they had stopped here before, the foreman had not been too friendly.

Their trail then takes them back into the depths of the forest and across a creek. Linz remembered, this was the stone bridge where they had first come across

Hendon, the strange forest dweller who can talk with nature.

It was not until later that they discovered they were all related via the D'Anjue bloodline, and that was Hendon's special skill bestowed upon him by the stones of Berghein. Linz's skill was more subtle, never realizing he had it for most of his life as it seemed so natural. He could sense how to find things or trails that were important, so he knew he would be needed on the quest to search for the Duchess.

His duties to his people would have to wait. His mother, trusted and admired by the Lake people, would rule well in his absence. Hopefully the quest would be a short one and he could return to resume his duties. The Lake people were learning the history of their ancestral link to the D'Anjue family. Blood ties are always important to his tribe, so he felt certain they would approve of his mission.

A few hours later they arrived at the log house that was Hendon's home, but there were no signs of anyone there. The door was not locked and the insides looked undisturbed. The bed had not been slept in for a while.

"Maybe he goes to see new Queen," Wyatt suggested.

"That's exactly what I was thinking, Wyatt, and if two of us think this, I believe it must be so. We will sleep here tonight and rest the horses." He was certain that Hendon would not deny them the shelter of his home. "First thing in the morning we will depart for Castle Villeroy. I must relay my news to the Queen before she organizes a wider search for the Duchess."

***

Hendon sat in his room. He always missed the forest whenever he had to leave his home. The castle gardens were pretty enough, but they did not compare with the tall trees and the wild animals of his home in the Cefinon forest.

He picked up his staff, turning it in his hands, feeling the rough wood under his fingertips. He was faced with a sudden vision of riding his horse, Bartok, out in the hills. This pleased him because he thought his horse magnificent, yet why had Bartok suddenly come into his mind? Hendon believed there was a reason for everything, nothing was coincidence. No one can change the call of nature or of events that happen in one's life. Each individual plays their part in the game of life and hopes that at the end of their journey, all will be well.

An old man's gravelly voice came into his head. "Well, go on then. How many times do I have to tell you?" the voice commanded of him.

"Tell me what?" Hendon said aloud. "Who are you and where are you hiding?" His eyes scanned the room for the person whom the voice belonged.

"Do you have to shout?" the voice cried back, inside of his head.

Hendon put his hands to his ears as the unknown voice echoed around in his head.

"Use your mind boy, don't yell at me with your mouth," the voice instructed.

"You mean you really are in my head?" Hendon asked, through his thoughts and not his mouth.

"That's much better. You take an awful long time to grasp things. I can see I will have my work cut out, training you."

"I don't even know who you are?" Hendon said, in his mind.

"Now listen, very carefully, I'm only going to explain this but once to you. Do you hear me, boy?"

Hendon did not reply. He smiled to himself. He had a good idea who he was having a conversation with, in his head.

"You will take me with you wherever you go. I am to be treated like one of your limbs, and also with the utmost of kindness, so no more polishing, it tickles," the gravelly voice said.

"I know exactly who you are," Hendon said. "I think you've turned into a miserable old man in the spirit world, Barnaby, as you sound very grumpy in death."

"Hmmph, that's as may be, but don't you be getting above your station. This is the only way I can help, now that my body has passed away. I didn't like the thing anyway, it was full of aches and pains," the voice said, not denying it was Barnaby.

"To what purpose would you wish to linger on in this world, Barnaby?"

"Until the balance is set again. Now then listen, you must go to the lizard people for two reasons. First, you can rescue the Duchess, whom I happen to have a great fondness for. Then you can set to rights what needs to be done. Now go off and tell the Queen. I need to rest now. I can't communicate with you for long. Off you go, boy."

With that he was gone, and Hendon was once again left in peace.

CHAPTER 5

There was a commotion outside of Hendon's rooms, which overlooked the stable's courtyard. Crossing the room to peer out of the window, he saw that Linz had arrived with one of his tribesmen. He knew that the Queen had not sent for him. She had said she felt he had enough responsibilities with his new role as Chief. So it was a mystery as to why he was here.

He had always liked Linz, strong and determined despite his young years, he instantly felt better knowing he was here. With his exceptional skills at tracking, he would be useful in their quest. Especially now they had a destination. Picking up his staff he went to greet the new arrival. As Hendon arrived in the courtyard, Linz was still in the stable mounted on his horse, as was his companion.

"Ah, Linz, good to see you, my friend. You have arrived at a good time. You must have known that we needed you," he said as he approached the young Lake chief who was now dismounting from his horse.

"Hendon," Linz smiled at the approaching forest dweller. Their hands clasped together in a friendly greeting. "I have news for the Queen," he told him.

"I will come to see her with you, as I too have news to convey," he said, dropping his voice to almost a whisper and staring at Linz's companion who stood close by.

"This is my faithful guard, Wyatt," Linz introduced his riding partner. "He is also my teacher for I have much to learn in combat. You can trust him. I do, with my life."

Hendon felt satisfied at this and continued his conversation. "We must go on a journey to the Lizard people. Who is better to negotiate with them than the Chief of the Lake people. Indeed, you must have sensed that we needed you."

Linz was momentarily stunned by Hendon's words. It seemed the dream was an omen after all. He stepped closer to his friend and recounted his nightmare to him.

"I had a terrible vision one night." Linz was now also whispering. "I knew it was more than a normal dream. The lizard people had murdered the Duchess. I feel the dream was an omen and I agree that we need to go on a journey and speak to these people. I do believe that is where the monk Ghaffar has taken her, but I don't know why."

Hendon looked on in horror at Linz's account of the dream. "Surely if the Duchess was dead, Myriam would know?"

"I cannot say, my friend," Linz replied, unable to offer any comfort. "I'm not sure if what I have seen has happened, or is yet to come to pass."

They were both so deeply engrossed in their conversation that neither of them had heard Ganry approach.

"So, it seems that Myriam's perceptions are becoming strong," a gravelly voice sounded across the stables. Both looked towards the sound of the voice and watched the veteran warrior approach. He had been sent by Myriam to greet Linz as she had felt his presence close by, even though she had no knowledge that he had arrived.

"Let's not keep the Queen waiting. She is keen to hear your news Linz, and why you felt it so urgent to leave your people in their time of need," Ganry stated.

Myriam was so pleased to see Linz that she could not help herself but run to him, and hugged him tightly in her greeting. Ganry looked on and frowned, *one day,* he thought to himself, s*he will behave like a Queen*, but he said nothing. Myriam had much on her mind and small issues of formalities were the least of her worries.

"I know it hasn't been long since last we met, but when we're together I feel such a strong bond," she explained to all present. "We have much to discuss. I'm sure you have both had a message of sorts with regards to the quest to find my grandmother?" she asked, awaiting an answer.

"I had a terrible dream," Linz replied first, "and it involved the Rooggaru, or at least his race."

Myriam shuddered at her memory of their encounter with the large lizard. They were lucky to escape with their lives that day, indeed they almost lost Ganry. The thought of having to face a whole race of those lizard people filled her with dread.

"Legend says that they gave the stones to our ancestors to enable us to battle with their long hated enemy, the dragons," Myriam said. "It could be just that though, a legend. Truly I do not know where the Berghein stones came from, though my tutor, Leonidavus, came from Berghein, so I suppose there must be a connection with that area. I do not see how the lizard people owned those stones, other than they may have stolen them. This would not surprise me as I do not trust these creatures. Do you really believe that our quest means we have to deal with this terrible race?"

"I agree with Linz, Myriam. My staff also told me we must journey to the Rooggaru," Hendon said.

All looked at the staff in his hand, but no one spoke of it. With everything they had experienced recently, a talking staff did not seem so fantastical. Only Ganry looked skeptical.

"I too have had a dream," Myriam informed them. "My grandmother came to me to let me know that she still lives. She also mentioned the Berghein stones and urged me to keep them close, and not give them up because our powers will fade." She paused, waiting to see if anyone could shed light on her conundrum. When no one spoke she continued, "It's a real puzzle to me. Why would we give up the stones?"

Still no reply from her friends. She felt that the answer to this question was essential to their success, but it remained a mystery.

"Let's catch up over dinner," she suggested. "Linz, you can take the room next to Hendon's. I think the sooner we all talk together, the better. My grandmother is very precious to this bloodline. As the Queen, I want to thank her for all the help she provided me in gaining back my throne. Go and clean up Linz, you've had a long journey. I will see you both at dinner," she finished.

All bowed and left the Queen's chambers, with the exception of Ganry.

"You have a kingdom to run, my Queen. Think wisely before embarking on quests that others can do for you."

Then he too, bowed and left the room.

CHAPTER 6

They all met at dinner where they listened intently to Hendon's explanation. "I don't know why none of you can hear him when he's so clear to me. Though he does speak in riddles and I don't always understand his words."

Everyone was gathered around Hendon's staff, because he had told them that Barnaby communicated with him through the strange piece of wood. Barnaby himself, found it all rather amusing but refused to perform at Hendon's command.

No one else can hear, foolish boy, because I speak in your head. Barnaby thought that if he had a head, he would be shaking it right now.

"I still maintain it's just a piece of wood with some carvings on it. There is no such thing as magic," Ganry said, sounding like he was trying to convince himself more than anything else.

"He tells me that the lizard subterranean city lies in Vandemland," Hendon continued, ignoring Ganry's comment. "That is where we must go if we are to save the Duchess."

"Do you know how big that country is?" Ganry said, shaking his head in disbelief. "Where does your stick suggest we start?"

"I think we should go to Qutaybah," Myriam suggested. "He proved to be very faithful to my grandmother's cause. He will help us find her once he knows she is still missing. I'm sure he will."

"Queen Myriam, I understand your concerns for the Duchess, but I feel I must advise you that this is no quest for a Queen." Ganry once again made his opposition to this folly be known.

Myriam knew that she really needed to learn to exert herself better with Ganry. He was her protector and she trusted him and his advice, but she was the Queen, she needed to have the final decision in everything.

"This is not just any quest, Ganry, this is my grandmother, who, might I remind you, saved my crown. I cannot leave it to others to find her and bring her home. I owe her too much."

"She is right, Ganry." Linz felt he also needed to help the Duchess, despite his responsibilities. "I too should not have left my leadership in another's hands, but the Duchess is kin. Because of her the Lake people now own their lands, officially. We no longer need to stay a secret tribe. We owe her much, as does Myriam."

"Artas, Hendon, have you two any more to add to this argument?" Ganry pleaded with them for their opinions. If he could sway half the group to his view, then perhaps he could get Myriam to remain at the castle and rule her kingdom, as she was meant to.

Artas spoke first. "I lost my parents to that usurper, Duke Harald. I cannot take my revenge out on the false Regent because he is dead. What I can do is honor the one person who made sure that happened. I say the entire kingdom owes the Duchess this favor."

Ganry knew he could not argue with that because it was true. The Duchess had been the only noble to fight the usurper to start with. Her bravery was probably what encouraged the others to finally make their move. He also realized, and was secretly quite pleased, that Myriam had a steely resolve about her, one that he could not sway. It boded well for her future reign, should she survive this expedition.

"I would not stop you. Your very wish is my command," Ganry replied, resignedly. "If you are to go, then so shall I, of that I am steadfast."

An uneasy silence fell on the room while each contemplated the decisions that were being made. It was Hendon who finally broke the stillness.

"There is more I haven't yet told you." He waited to be sure he had everyone's attention before continuing. "I cannot tell you for certain what it is, but there is more to this quest than a simple rescue. Barnaby gave me one of his warnings in a riddle: *They want that of which we own, so we must beware.*"

"What? What do we own that they want, Hendon? I do not understand these words. Surely if we knew what is was we could deal with this much quicker?"

"That, my Queen, I do not know," Hendon replied, humbly. "My staff, or rather the spirit within it, speaks in riddles. I sometimes think he is playing games with me."

"It is clear to me that all immediate members of the D'Anjue bloodline need to be on this journey," Linz added. "We have all had a message of sorts. I had a dream, Hendon has his voice in a stick, and-"

"A staff, Linz, it is not merely a stick," Hendon interrupted.

"Through your staff," Linz corrected, seeing it was important to his friend. "And, Myriam has had a message from her grandmother, the Duchess, through a dream. We are destined to follow this path together."

"It is decided then," Queen Myriam said, forcibly, ensuring that Ganry was in no doubt of her determination to get her own way on this. "There will be myself, and Ganry to protect me. Linz and his protector, Wyatt. Plus Hendon. We five will travel to Vandemland and return the Duchess safely back to her homeland, though her castle lays in ruins since it was burned to the ground."

Someone grunted a throaty cough in the background and all eyes turned in their direction.

"Aren't you forgetting someone?" Artas spoke up.

"No, Artas I had not forgotten you, for you will stand in my stead as Regent. You of all the people I know, I can trust."

"I thought you were going in secret?" Artas pointed out.

"That secret will soon be uncovered when we go. I would need to inform the Heads of State and politicians anyway, and not one of those could be trusted to keep a confidence. No, our absence will soon be noted by the interfering decision makers. This way, should the people find out I go in search of my grandmother, you will be here to keep order. Artas, I know you wish to come along, but equally the kingdom needs an honest leader." She would not force this upon her personal knight, but he really was the best candidate to hold the fort.

"Yes, my Queen, it will be my honor to care for your kingdom in your absence." Despite his heavy sadness at not going on the rescue mission, he managed to disguise his disappointment. "Although once my injury is healed, I'm coming along on the any other adventures."

"Absolutely, Artas," Myriam smiled and hugged him.

"So, that's decided then." Myriam was relieved it had all gone her way. She really was going to enjoy being Queen. "We set off as soon as we are fully prepared, and certainly within the next few days."

All returned to their quarters to rest before the journey began, and each would reflect on their roles in the mission. Ganry was determined that Myriam would return to rule her kingdom, even if that meant he had to lay down his own life to ensure her safe return.

CHAPTER 7

The five travelers decided to journey in disguise while they were still in the Kingdom of Palara, each one wearing the simple clothes of merchants. Each would also carry a small supply of silks to reinforce their deception.

Having horses meant they could carry plenty of food supplies and hide their weapons from prying eyes. After much discussion, they agreed that a wagon would slow them down, although Ganry would have preferred one as it would have allowed them to hide the Queen.

Since the coupe, there was now much more trade activity. Myriam's new advisors had agreed to slacken security on all borders. They hoped this would lead to an increase in trade to help the crown pay for the cost of the war that the usurper had caused. Trade negotiations were just one of many new changes that Myriam had implemented. Trade would bring prosperity back to the people of Palara.

This night they were staying at an inn just a mile from the borders of Vandemland. It was a busy inn due to the borders being overcrowded. The pass between the two kingdoms was set on a narrow road, between high cliffs. Prior to the coup, hardly anyone had used the official posts to cross the border, with smugglers having free reign. Now the borders were better patrolled and most, if not all, goods had to go through the official crossings.

"Getting over the pass isn't the problem," Ganry informed the group over their venison dinner. "It's finding the elusive Qutaybah that is proving difficult. The Duchess had an alliance with him, but no other in the kingdom has such a privilege. I can send word by the Narcs, but this will be costly and even then they are not trustworthy. They are known as the smugglers, but the opening of the borders has made smuggling useless so they will now be looking for other ways to be making money."

"I heard of a terrible tale told by the castle guards about the Narcs," Myriam disclosed. "They sold Captain Henrickson and his squire, Arexos, into slavery. They had gone as spies sent by my uncle. You know, he was planning to invade Vandemland once he had the crown. He was totally mad," she told the others, but none had known of the usurpers intentions. Ganry had always ignored the nobles and definitely had no time for politicians. "It's true," she emphasized with wide eyes. "The worse part of the tale is that Arexos managed to get back to the castle and my uncle had him beheaded. Poor boy. It seems my uncle was murdering people at a fast pace. He would have made a terrible

King. I cannot imagine the state of the kingdom with his rule. My father was far too trusting of his brother."

The Queen's friends remained silent. Myriam rarely spoke of the coup. They all knew that the grief from losing both parents was still fresh and painful. Ganry felt she never had the chance to grieve her losses, but what did he know of a young girl's needs. He had lost his own daughter at a similar age to Myriam, so his role at fatherhood had been thwarted. This was all the more reason to rescue the Duchess. Myriam needed a mother figure to help her mature, and to guide her into being a "good and just" Queen for the kingdom.

Everyone in the party slept lightly that night. Tomorrow they would brave the crossing into Vandemland.

They all rose early, whilst the sky was still in darkness, and ate a light breakfast before setting off. Reaching the border crossing just as the sun was rising above the horizon, it seemed that they were not the only ones looking for an early start.

"We could get through the thronging crowd much quicker if we told them who you really are," Hendon suggested, looking in dismay at the long line of people trying to get over the border. This was going to slow down their progress.

"We cannot let the kingdom know that the Queen endangers herself in foreign lands," Ganry said. "It's mad enough that she's here, but it is essential she remains incognito."

"On this one, I agree with Ganry," Myriam put in. "Can we not bribe our way forward? A few coins here and there to push our way to the front of the line?"

"It is a viable option," Ganry agreed. "We will pose as the Johannson family once again, as we did in the town of Athaca. Myriam can be a sickly daughter that we are keen to get home quickly. Linz and Hendon can choose the people to bribe in the line so we can move forward to the border guards at a quicker pace."

It did not prove that easy a task. Many of the people in the line were traders, all equally in a rush to sell their goods at local markets. It was easier for Linz and Hendon to offer to buy their wares, as the traders understood this far better than just receiving the money for nothing, which made them uneasy and suspicious.

"I will buy your knife, at a good rate, but only if you let my family have your place in the line," Linz bartered with the a large man, stood in front of them.

It was a slow trade but it was moving them down the line quicker. Ganry and Wyatt stayed on their horses, observing for anything suspicious. Ganry had come to like Wyatt. He was much older in years than Linz and a veteran in battle. It seemed all in the line had learned of the family with the weak daughter and they all expected the trade deals to take place as the Johannson family arrived behind them.

After a few hours, Ganry was the next to be questioned by the border guards. He worried that the guards may have heard of their trickery to get to the front of the line, but it seemed that the tradespeople did not communicate with the guards unless they had to. It seemed to be an accepted opinion of, "them," and "us." The Johannson family were through the border guards in no time, with their purses much lighter and their saddles laden with the bartered goods.

They entered the first town after crossing the border and Ganry led them to an inn.

"We will be approached by a guide, sent to us from the Narcs. He is to take us to see Qutaybah," Ganry explained.

They all settled down and awaited the guides arrival. Qutaybah was a mysterious figure to most of them. They had heard he was a rich man, a hardened slaver and mercenary, hiring out his private army to the best payers. What they were certain of though, was that no one should ever cross him. The plains of Vandemland were littered with the graves of those who had dared.

CHAPTER 8

Artas was disappointed that he had not been able to go with the Queen on her quest. He was supposed to be her personal knight, an honor he had taken seriously. It seemed this was not a role that was needed all of the time, especially when she had Ganry. However, Ganry was older than him, so he supposed he would be trained to take his place, eventually.

Smiling at that thought, he looked down at the crowd that stood before him. One of his roles in the Queen's absence was to placate the nobles. He was to convince them that the Queen was unwell and unavailable. There were few who were privy to the fact that she was not even in the castle, but the others must be told that he was Regent, given this role by his Queen.

He understood them to be nervous of a Regent, so soon after the cruel, vindictive self appointed Harald who had only recently held this position. But they could not compare him to Duke Harald. The man had murdered his parents by beheading them. He could never be a merciless leader, only a just one. He intended on doing a good job, while the Queen was absent. She had bestowed much responsibility on him, so he would forget the quest and meet his role head on.

Standing up, he took in a deep breath and then yelled at the top of his voice, surprising himself just how loud he was capable of shouting.

"My Lords, it is time for silence!" he ordered them. "I have been given the task of relaying all your concerns to your Queen. You are given the task of patience, and I see no sign of that amongst any of you today."

Now he had their attention, he would instruct them of the Queen's wishes.

"We have just finished a war. Our kingdom is in no hurry to be making rash decisions. The people need peace for a while, not changes. You must understand what your Queen has gone through. Now we must leave her to grieve her parents, let her have a mourning period. I'm sure even the politicians amongst you understand this human need.

"I will act as her representative. All your messages will be relayed to our Queen and all unimportant decisions can wait. I will be announcing to the citizens of the Kingdom of Palara that there is going to be a period of mourning for King Ludwig and Queen Alissia. It is only respectful and proper that we put them in our thoughts, even if only for a short while. That includes nobles and politicians."

With the end of his speech, he bowed to the frowning faces and made his leave. He would have to face them again the next day, but for the rest of today, he would avoid them like a plague.

The Queen had called upon one of her faithful nobles, the young Lord Parsival of Ival Hold. He had been one of the first to come to her aid and had even attempted to assassinate Harald. For his troubles he had been incarcerated in the castle's dungeons and no doubt treated with cruelty.

Since his release, once the throne was taken back by the rightful owner, she had come to trust his judgment. Artas also liked Lord Parsival and was glad for his council. Together they would run the Kingdom in the Queen's absence.

"Bravo, Artas," Parsival greeted him as he arrived back from his meeting with the nobles and politicians. "I heard your speech, very authoritative. That should placate them for a day or two."

Artas smiled as he received the liquor that Parsival had poured for him in a beautifully cut glass goblet. It burned his throat and made his toes tingle, but it hit the spot.

"I think we're going to be needing a few of those over the next few months," Artas declared.

"Fear not, Artas, for we are not alone," Parsival assured him. "There are few nobles that the Queen truly trusts, but there are enough of us to carry this deception through for a short while. No harm will come to her Kingdom and she shall rule all the better for having her grandmother by her side. Relax, the first day is over and all has gone as planned."

Artas sat in a large cushioned chair and remembered his lost friend, Zander, who had been killed by a dragon on their quest to try and rid the land of Harald the usurper. Zander had been Duchess D'Anjue's Chief Advisor, and he wished he were here now, to advise Artas.

Whilst he knew he had trusted nobles on his side, ultimately all decisions were to be on his head. Myriam must truly trust him to have ordained him Regent, and this thought cheered him. Though they had played together as children, and adventured together as adults, they were yet to spend time together socially.

He looked forward to Myriam's return once her grandmother was safe. It would be a time for peace and relaxation. That time would come soon. He just needed the patience that he had asked of the nobles.

Lady Leonie walked into the room. She was also one of his loyal advisors. It was a pleasure to watch her enter the room so gracefully, for she was a beautiful and cultured lady.

"How are you both bearing up?" she asked, knowing Parsival would be fine, but also that Artas was still grieving his parents death. He rarely showed his grief, but Leonie knew him well and could still see the pain of loss in his eyes.

Leonie too had attempted to assassinate the false Regent, along with Parsival, and like him she had spent a while in the dungeons. It was about that failed attempt that she was here now as she had recently learned of who the betrayer had been on the eve of the assassination attempt.

"I cannot see how the news I have to tell you should affect our temporary running of the Kingdom, but I do believe that Parsival deserves to know who betrayed us."

This had Parsival's attention and he stood up. He had often wondered who could have known, other than the loyal nobles involved, and none of them would have sided with the usurper.

"It was the monk, the one that you said was last seen with the Duchess. I found out from one of the guards who was posted with Duke Harald. He was there during one of his conversations with the strange little man," Leonie finished.

"You mean, Ghaffar?"

Leonie simply nodded.

CHAPTER 9

Queen Myriam had only met Qutaybah once, and that had been fleeting. After she had regained her throne, she had never really had the chance to thank him, for she knew he had played a part as he was allied with her grandmother.

He took her hand in greeting as they arrived in one of his many homes. He had specifically chosen this one as it was nearest to the border. His large dark skinned hand encompassed hers, delicate and pale in contrast.

"Any who are aligned to the Duchess D'Anjue are welcome in my home and in my lands. I will provide you with safe passage, Queen Myriam, for I wish to see the Duchess back in her homelands," he said. "My only regret is that I did not secure her safety before I left your Kingdom. I had not realized that she had been taken."

"Nor we," Myriam responded, annoyed at herself for not seeking out her grandmother as soon as she had arrived back at the castle. Though she had probably been long gone by then. "We had word that she had been released from the dungeon and I think we all presumed her safe. The sly monk had slipped her away from under my nose, and I will have her returned at all costs."

"Please, let us sit and eat," Qutaybah opened up his arms, welcoming the small party to be seated upon the plush cushions. He gestured at a table where a variety of fruits, cheeses, meats, plus servants, awaited upon their pleasure.

All took a seat with the exception of Ganry. He was always on duty to protect his Queen, even if this Qutaybah was meant to be an ally. Ganry would eat when his Queen slept. For now, he would listen and observe. Later he would learn much information from the gossiping slaves and servants.

"I have heard of this Ghaffar, he is an elusive creature. He dwells in the forbidden lands of the underground dwellers. We call them the Akkedis Mense. My country has many riches under its soils and most of it is mined, but the forbidden lands are never entered by the wise. This is where the Akkedis Mense dwell and none would wish to stir up their nests. Ghaffar is a chameleon. He can disguise himself as many creatures. Your people have seen him as a monk, mine have seen him as a rich merchant. Whatever disguise he wears, he is a reptilian by heart. He is an ambassador of his people, the Akkedis Mense."

"You have given us much information to ponder, Qutaybah, I thank you for your openness," Myriam said.

"My people are familiar with a legend of the Rooggaru, which you call Akkedis Mense," Linz spoke up, remembering what had happened the night he lost his uncle. "Ghaffar had one of these creatures with him whilst he lived at the temple near my home. It was a vile and vicious monster and killed Chief Clay by draining him of his blood. If Ghaffar is a Rooggaru, or Akkedis Mense, then I do not think he can be trusted."

"We may have something that he wants," Hendon spoke. "Why else would he take the Duchess other than to lure us there to rescue her?"

"He seemed a kind man when he brought my grand-mother's men to me. They had been searching for me in vain until he showed them the way. I believe whatever he wants must be connected to the D'Anjue bloodline," Myriam shared her thoughts. "I also believe it must be something we are loathe to give up, otherwise he would have just asked us, surely?" she added.

"Well," Ganry finally said, wanting this meeting to end, "we won't know until we meet them in person, and as the journey there is long and perilous I suggest an early night."

He hoped this would encourage Myriam to see that there was no more to be learned here, and retire to her rooms. There she would be safely in once place, and he could mingle amongst the household to find out any real secrets. Slaves do not do the bidding of their masters, voluntarily. A few coins in the right direction and he should find out all he needed to know.

He glanced over at Qutaybah. He was fearsome looking, very powerfully built and completely bald. Ganry did not trust him despite his proclamation of friendship to his Queen. Having been a mercenary himself, he knew that his sword had gone to the highest bidder. What if this bald man was playing both sides? What if he was just luring them into a trap? The sooner they were away from here, the happier he would feel.

"I personally cannot guarantee your safety, Queen Myriam," Qutaybah's deep, rumbling voice said. "Instead, I will send one of my most trusted guards with you. I would like to introduce you to Perseus. He is to be your guide while you are traveling in this region, and he will take you deep into the forbidden lands where many of my people do not dare to tread."

Ganry looked at the huge warrior who had just entered the room. He was nearly twice the size of himself. He wondered at how much his role was meant to be as a spy, and how much as a guide. He knew that their guide would be doing Qutaybah's bidding, and not theirs.

"Perseus is a welcome addition to our group of travelers," Myriam thanked Qutaybah, for she knew they could not do this quest without his help. "Once again, my family owes you thanks for the kindness that you show us."

Myriam was not fooled by Qutaybah's kindness. She knew it would come at a price, but her grandmother could negotiate that once she was free, for this was her ally.

Linz was awed by the huge warrior, Perseus. So much so that he could not resist getting up from his seat to prod him, and check if he was real.

"I think with Ganry, Wyatt and Perseus, we will be unbeatable indeed," Linz laughed, and he was not without his own skills when it came to battle. He felt secure that Myriam would be safe in the hands of such companions.

Hendon played no part in the amusement of the new group member. Instead he would be relying on his magic, not his muscles, which could not be compared to the fighters in the group. But, nor could any of them talk to the animals and to nature itself. Since accepting the Berghein stones as his bloodline right, his skills had been enhanced to such levels that he would never want to be without his magic ever again.

"That's settled then," Queen Myriam announced. "We are now a group of six. My grandmother will be most grateful upon her return."

With this Myriam stood and said her goodbyes, agreeing that Ganry would organize their departure with Perseus so that they could all leave the next morning.

CHAPTER 10

"Has the Duchess been treated badly?" Ghaffar asked, knowing the answer already.

"Ghaffar, you know perfectly well that your people are treating me with the utmost respect. What I'm trying to convey to you is that you have gone about this in the wrong manner."

"Are you saying that had I asked you for the Berghein stones back, you would have willingly given them, knowing that your magical skills will be weakened?"

"That depends upon your reasoning as to why we must return these stones. Do you have proof that it was your people who gave the stones to the D'Anjue ancestors in the first place?"

The Duchess was always open to reasoning, but Ghaffar had provided none, and she could not know whether he simply coveted the stones for underhand reasons. Besides, descendants of her bloodline had only recently found all the Berghein stones and brought them together. They would not give them up easily, especially as a D'Anjue now served on the throne.

These stones would help prevent any more attempts to unseat the true heir. They would protect Myriam and any heirs she produces. How can this little man, who calls himself a monk, expect her family to simply hand over the stones to them?

"My sources inform me that, indeed, your family are on their way to rescue you. They must love you dearly," Ghaffar said, and then promptly bowed as he left the room.

"Obnoxious little man," the Duchess mumbled to herself.

Since she had been brought to this strange place, she had no other company other than her own, so she was inclined to talk to herself. It helped her think things through. There was something he was not telling her but she had yet to find out what it was.

The problem at the moment was her forgetfulness, although she often associated it with her old age, plus all that she had gone through recently, she also knew she was not usually so bad. She vaguely remembered Ghaffar convincing her to leave with him, but she could not remember why, and now she felt certain that she was being kept here against her will.

The door was locked all the time and she saw no one but the monk. He had treated her well enough and healed the injuries she had received from being tortured, but yet she still felt a sickness deep inside. Something was wrong but she could not determine exactly what it was. She had endured much pain to allow her granddaughter to escape. Never would she begrudge

Myriam her freedom at the price of her torture, but now that she was Queen, she had hoped that Myriam would send someone to her rescue.

Not trusting the monk, Ghaffar, it left her with no one to confide in. All she could do was wait for events to unfold and hope that this would all be resolved soon, as it seemed a party was on its way to her. She hoped that Myriam had stayed in Palara as she felt certain there were dangers here for the Queen should she come herself.

Always, she felt a claustrophobia in this catacomb of a city. The rooms were large and the city was well developed, but at the end of the day there was no fresh air to breath. The only ventilation that lingered was what had managed to filter through the built in network of airway tunnels. Even lizards needed to breath air to survive.

Feeling tired as she always seemed to be these days, she lay her head down and was soon in a fitful slumber. In her sleep she tossed and turned, dreaming of her blood seeping away from her body. It was a fitful rest, and she was glad to awaken and find herself still alive.

Yet, it was always the same when she woke up from the dream, she had a sense that she had not been alone. She always sensed that someone had come into her room and had left before she awoke. Why she sensed this, she did not know, but she felt it was a part of the reason as to why she was here.

This time, she knew someone was in the room and when she awakened, they were still there. She saw it was a female lizard. She could just make it out in the shadows and knew it was a female as they smelled more pleasanter than the males, who had a distinctly unpleasant sour odor.

The female spoke to another in the room but the Duchess could not see very well and felt light headed. Nor could she understand the language of these lizard people.

"*She has awoken early,*" the female said in her own tongue, knowing that the human would not understand her words. "*Shall I drug her some more?*"

"*No, take what blood you have to our Empress, that will placate her for now,*" a voice replied in the same language. She recognized it as belonging to Ghaffar. "*I will deal with the consequences,*" he assured the female who was quite concerned she did not have a full cup of blood.

A voice called her name and the Duchess was somewhat confused as to where she was. As of late she was getting weaker, not stronger.

"Duchess D'Anjue," there was the voice again. "Are you well?"

The Duchess peered into the dim room to see the little monk looming over her. She sat up with a start.

"How long have you been present in my room while I rest?" she demanded.

"Your voice could be heard calling out, so I was sent to check in on your safety. I think you were having a dream, Duchess," Ghaffar explained. "I have brought you refreshment. You must keep up your strength."

He passed her a glass containing a warm liquid which she drank gratefully. She was never certain what this cup contained, but he had explained once that it was a mix of local herbs which helped to build strength. Whatever it was she always felt better after taking it.

She passed him back the glass and laid her head back onto the pillow, her eyes heavy again. She meant to ask him who the other person had been in the room with them, but it did not seem important anymore as a warm feeling swept over her, easing her worries.

Ghaffar smiled as the Duchess slipped back into slumber. He contemplated for a moment calling the servant girl back in to finish the blood draining, but decided against it. The Empress would have to make do with less tonight. There would be plenty to come in the future. If his spies were to be believed then the whole remaining bloodline of the D'Anjue were making their way to them.

Yes, soon she would have all the blood she needed to survive her next transformation.

CHAPTER 11

The group had traded their horses for camels as this creature was more suited for the new terrain they had to cross. Myriam liked her camel, who was called Al Bikra, because she had not mated yet. She was one of the two humps variety which made riding her more comfortable. Al Bikra was partial to dates, and whoever fed her them would receive her loyalty. With this in mind, Myriam always had a pocket full of the sticky fruit at the ready.

The others in the group were not so lucky. Ganry's was a seasoned camel but also a little on the feisty side, not always doing what Ganry commanded. Each camel had its own character, just as the horses at home, only camels were proving a little moodier.

Perseus led the train of camels who seemed happy to walk in single line as they progressed through the dry arid landscape. They were heading towards a large desert area which should take them onto the forbidden lands where the Akkedis Mense ruled.

They passed by many mines where it appeared that the workers were slaves. Myriam's parents had disapproved of such practices, and after witnessing the cruelty of the poor workers, Myriam vowed she would never allow this in her Kingdom.

It was clear that these people were worked to the death and she wondered if they were perhaps prisoners. She must remember to ask Perseus about slavery and see if it was something her own people could find the power to stop, especially if trade was strong. Maybe they could bring in laws that nothing could be traded if slavery was involved in the process.

Vandemland was famous for its rare and precious gems, so surely it could afford to pay their workers. Myriam felt strongly about this and was determined to do her very best to ensure none of her trading partners used slavery.

"You are deep in your thoughts," Ganry's voice interrupted her planning.

"I don't like to see people used in this way, Ganry. Look at them. Many seem near death. Why do the leaders of this land allow such cruelty?" she quizzed him, knowing he was a man of much experience.

Hendon then rode up by her other side as he had overheard her comments.

"Artas told me that Duke Harald sent over his Captain of the Guard as a spy, but he was sold into slavery. He was put to death at one of the mines for attempting to escape. It did not come to light until after the battle. Border guards had heard tell of the tale from a merchant called Ragnald. He had informed the slave guards of Captain Henrickson's attempted escape and he was let free for being so loyal. Mind you, I've also heard tell that once a slave you will never be freed. Terrible business," Hendon concluded.

"You have much to say on this matter, Hendon," Myriam smiled. "I believe we agree on this and perhaps upon our return we can approach the politicians to put pressure on such practices. If anything, maybe we can improve conditions for these poor people."

"It would take hundreds of years for such changes to happen," Ganry said. "It is the way of these people. Concern yourself with your own lands, Myriam, not those beyond your control."

Queen Myriam said no more on the subject, but she would not forget.

Most nights they camped out but occasionally they arrived at one of Qutaybah's properties. They were due to stop at one for this night and Myriam looked forward to sleeping in a real bed. It's not that she wasn't used to sleeping outside, she had spent many a rough night on the roads when she was escaping the clutches of her cruel uncle. Still, it did not mean that she could not enjoy the comforts of a soft bed and pillows, and maybe even a means of bathing. These luxuries were all the more enjoyable since she had lived life on the run.

The building was only a single storey, but it was large as it seemed to spread out over the land. Most buildings they had passed in these parts were painted in white because of the heat. This was no different. They arrived into a courtyard where servants received them and relieved them of their burdens. Food was supplied in abundance.

Myriam wondered if these servants were also slaves. If they were, then their lot was much better than the ones she had seen in the mines. These looked healthy and well fed, yet how could anyone live happily if they were not free to chose their own way in life?

Too tired to approach Perseus, she simply ate a light meal and went to her rooms where, luckily, a bath tub full of warm water awaited. Soaking her aching body in such comfort and ridding her skin and hair of road dust, it seemed that all was well with the world. What could possibly go wrong?

CHAPTER 12

At dinner that very evening, Myriam brought up the subject of slavery with Perseus.

"I'm curios, Perseus, to know if the people who work for Qutaybah are slaves?"

Perseus had proved to be a man of few words, so she was surprised at the lengthy explanation he gave.

"Are not we all slaves in some way, Queen Myriam? We all try to live our lives as best we can, but we must eat and clothe ourselves and our families. We must have a roof over our heads. We all need these rewards for the work that we perform. I understand the concept may be difficult, but most enter slavery willingly for the security it provides them, and there are other advantages too. In my homeland slaves are not allowed to wander freely or unaccompanied, this helps in reducing crime. Is this not a good thing?"

Myriam did not answer straight away as he had made some good points. As she ate her food, she contemplated on his words. It would not do to rush at a reply and yet have no reasoning behind her argument.

"Yes, Perseus," she spoke so all could hear. "In a sense we all must slave to provide the necessities of life, such as food and shelter, but that is not slavery to a master, that is slavery to a system. A slave who is purchased by a cruel master will not care about rewards, indeed, I do not think those poor people in the mines were hardly even fed."

"Those in the mines are often the criminals of society, but others do end up there as well, this is true," Perseus admitted. "My own master rewards his slaves well, but yes, we do belong to him."

"Wouldn't you like to travel to other places, yourself, Perseus?"

"I do travel, when my master instructs me, and I do see other places, Queen," he replied.

She understood Perseus to be loyal to Qutaybah, his master, so she would not question him further, it would not be fair. This was something she had to live with as a Queen of a people who have freedom. It would take many, many years to forge changes, but she hoped her legacy in years to come would be that of the Queen who opposed slavery in all its forms.

For now she had other matters and events that needed to be dealt with immediately, and could not wait.

"Perseus, I appreciate your honesty," she smiled at him. "Tell me, do you have a family?"

Perseus was uncomfortable with this line of questioning, but he knew she was a Queen and his master had impressed upon him how important the Duchess was to him. So, he must take great care of this grand-daughter to the Duchess that his master praised so highly.

"I have no family, Queen, I serve only my master." With that he stood, bowed and left the room.

Myriam tried not to look at Ganry immediately. She knew he would be scowling at her. Finally, she lifted her head and forced her eyes over to his battle hardened features.

"I am a Queen, I have to learn," she said to him. Then she herself stood and left the room, not giving Ganry the opportunity to reply.

"Our Queen is trying to understand the world around her," Hendon offered him.

Ganry said nothing. He too hated slavery, but it would take more than an idealist Queen to change the world.

Artas was pleased how his session with the merchants had gone. Most were complaining at the opening of the borders as the competition from bordering nations was forcing them to lower their prices. The influx of foreign traders did not sit well with the Palaran merchants, but the people of this nation would benefit from it and it was a masterstroke by Queen Myriam.

With one single decision the stores were full once again with an abundance of food, and the people were beginning to reap the benefits of her rule. As a concession to the local traders, he had agreed to tax imported goods which would increase the price to meet local prices. Artas knew this was not the answer, but equally, it meant he could have a good night's sleep tonight, with happy local traders not complaining in his ears.

All he had to do was hold the kingdom temporarily. Once Myriam returned with her retinue, she would have many advisors to help her make more permanent decisions about trading. For now, he simply wanted to find temporary solutions and he felt he had achieved this.

When he arrived in the main parlor, both Parsival and Lady Leonie were there already. It was time to catch up on the noble's gossip. Lady Leonie had already built an intricate network of spies in all levels of Palaran society. Artas thought she would be a great help to the Queen, as she would need such skills to run her kingdom.

"I hear tell the ladies are wanting the Queen to marry as soon as she's well again," Leonie informed them.

"Are they indicating who they wish this husband to be?" Artas asked, quite amused at their presumptions.

"Well, some think it should be you," she smiled at Artas, knowing that would amuse him. "Others say someone from Vandemland, in order to bring the neighbors closer together by the tying of our two great nations with a marital bond. It seems none were interested in the Queen's wishes. They say it should be a political marriage."

"From what I know of our new Queen, I don't think she'll be that easily persuaded," Parsival added.

"I would marry Myriam tomorrow if it would make her happy, but I don't think I'm the one she would chose," Artas said, a little sadness in his heart. "I'm happy just to be her personal knight. I imagine Ganry will train me for the role, and when he grows older, I will stand in his place."

"Ganry will never be too old to stand by his Queen. Even in his dying hours he will be at her side," Parsival said. "I fear you will have a long wait, my friend."

"Poor, poor Artas." Lady Leonie kissed his cheek. "I know you feel disappointed that the Queen left you behind, Artas, but I believe it's only because you don't have the D'Anjue bloodline. She has come to rely on Ganry, and when he returns he will help you in your training."

She felt that she had become good friends with Artas and liked him. He was young and brave and turning into a handsome man. She was no match for the Queen, who he clearly had his heart set on, but she believed she had more in common with Artas than Myriam had.

CHAPTER 13

After a good night's rest and a hearty breakfast, Myriam's party set off into the desert. The journey was hot and laborious. Myriam was thankful they had camels for the journey, otherwise it would have been impossible on foot.

Myriam held a cloth sun parasol over her head. It did not help against the relentless heat of the sun, but it did stop her skin burning from its harsh rays. She wondered how the camels could manage such high temperatures, but they seemingly coped well.

They made good progress despite the heat. The camels really deserved their name of ships of the desert, and all was going to plan until the tremors began. Myriam had heard of earthquakes where the ground rumbled and toppled buildings, but she was sure they did not happen in this land.

She could see Perseus stand upright on his camel, scanning the horizon as if he was looking for something. Ganry rode up next to him and they talked together. She assumed they were discussing the tremors and waited patiently for them to come and inform her of its cause.

"Can you feel it?" Hendon asked as he approached.

"Yes, do you know what it is?" she asked hopefully.

"It's the desert worms. They move beneath us. I have never seen them but I can hear them communicating with one another. They are oblivious of us. It is not us they seek, but the waters."

"Yet, my young Hendon, if they come across us they will not hesitate to eat us." Ganry came up behind them. "I've just been asking Perseus. They move in groups and the creatures are huge. They are carnivores and therefore dangerous to us. We should move quickly to a crag near to here. It will take us off course but the sands are dangerous whilst the desert worms are beneath us. We will be safe on the rocks where they will not be able to sense us."

"Why ever didn't he mention these dangers to us?" Myriam asked.

"I don't think we would want to know of all the dangers that lurk out in this desert. Only as, and when, they happen," Ganry told her.

She knew that Ganry feared nothing. In fact she had never met anyone as brave as her seasoned warrior. He always chose his words carefully so maybe he was right. It is best not to know all the horrors that may befall them on this journey, or they may never keep going forward.

Perseus took the lead and swung the camels away, where they all followed in a single line. He had warned them that they must remain quiet and only talk in whispers. The desert worms could sense noise, and until they were upon the rocks then they were all in peril

In the distance, Myriam could see the crag. It was a large black outcrop, seemingly in the middle of the desert as though it had been dropped there by some giant. Myriam could sense the tension in Perseus. He was constantly looking back, anxiously, and she realized they were all in mortal danger. She stared longingly at the rocks and wished them closer.

As the crag loomed before them, Myriam was beginning to believe they would all make it. Then suddenly, chaos exploded all around them. The worms had sensed them and whilst they were actually seeking water, they always craved for meat.

The carnage began.

Wyatt's camel was the first to fall. A huge worm reared out of the ground as the sands parted. Its high pitched screech was deafening and Wyatt seemed to somersault as his ride was lost. He landed some distance away from the monster.

As Myriam turned in her seat, she saw three hideous creatures rearing out of the sands. The monsters resembled giant worms, but their heads had huge gaping mouths that were filled with row upon row of razor sharp, serrated teeth, clearly well adapted to tearing meat to shreds before swallowing it.

Wyatt's camel had lost its footing, slipping into the hole that the worm had created when it reared off the ground. The creature hovered above the luckless camel, and in one swoop it darted in a downwards motion, its jaws clamping onto one of the camel's back legs. As the worm forced its great weight into a backwards motion, the leg ripped away from the body.

Wyatt took out his broad sword and hacked at the side of the worm's ugly body. A thick, yellow substance spurted in an upwards fountain from the injured beast. The monster cried out, seemingly requesting help, and others came to its aid before it disappeared back into the ground.

The poor camel was still alive and writhing around, emitting a pitiful cry of fear and pain. Maybe it also was crying out for assistance, but unfortunately for the poor beast, none came. All its cries managed to do was alert another monster to its presence.

A worm hole opened up to its side where a huge beast came rushing out, raising at least ten foot into the air, half-in and half-out of the sand. It dropped back down, its gaping jaws burying into the soft flesh of the camel, dragging it underground.

Blood seeped through the sand, turning it a crimson red as the other worms converged on the feast. This did not placate them though. If anything it made them worse. They now had the smell of blood and could sense that there was more to be had.

Perseus and Ganry struck the hind quarters of the remaining camels to speed them up. They had to get to the crag quickly, while the worms were preoccupied with the fallen camel. There was only a few more feet to go and soon the rest of them were safely on the rocks.

Myriam watched on in horror as she realized that Wyatt had been left behind. She could see him running for his life, but he still had some distance to go.

Ganry turned his camel around, intending to head back out, but one glance and he knew it was hopeless. He noticed the rippling sand and saw the worms were moving too fast. He was never going to make it.

Linz realized that his compatriot was in danger, and he readied his camel to ride out to help him. Ganry reached out and held Linz's beast in check by the reins.

"You cannot save him," Ganry said sadly. "To try would mean certain death."

Linz drew his sword from its scabbard and turned to the former mercenary. "Take your hands off of me." Linz could not stand by.

Ganry kept a firm grip on the reins. "I do not wish to see you die needlessly. We will need you if we are to be successful in this mission, but if your honor forces you to ride out to your death, then I will not forcibly stop you."

Myriam watched on, feeling helpless. She too wanted them to save Wyatt, but knew deep inside it was not possible. She laid her hand on Linz's arm.

"Please, Linz," she begged. "Please, I do not want to see another death today."

Linz looked on hopelessly as he saw his friend surrounded by the monsters. He watched as Wyatt turned to him and waved for him to stay there, and not to try to be a hero.

Wyatt stood firm as the ground below him opened up, and a desert worm with gaping jaws came rushing in an upwards motion out of the sands, grabbing him by the midriff before dragging him below ground. The other worms screeched in triumph before they too dived back into the sands to feed on their prey.

"Nooo!" Linz screamed out his grief, as his friend was taken by the creatures.

He watched, unable to tear his eyes away form the scene in front of him as the final moments of his friend's life were played out. The yellow tinge to the sand was now mixed with red as Wyatt's life blood seeped out of the ground. Linz's whole body was wracked with grief and he felt the stinging hot tears flooding down his cheeks.

CHAPTER 14

That evening was spent in absolute silence upon the coldness of the rocks. Linz sat and stared at the blood-stained sand where his friend had spent his last moments of life. Even in the pitch darkness his eyes found the spot. He made no attempt to sleep. This night he would grieve for his protector and trainer. Though he had no plans on how he could kill these beasts, tomorrow was the start of his life when he would plan revenge on every sand worm he was ever to meet.

Myriam slept restlessly. The cold, hard rock surface was uncomfortable, and the visions of Wyatt's death plagued her dreams. Her mind was in shock and her body exhausted. Losing Wyatt had made her realize just how dangerous this mission was. Despite Wyatt's death she was determined more than ever to continue. Wyatt would not die in vain. She would not return to Palara without her grandmother.

Although they stayed upon the crag in absolute silence, the sand worms did not leave. Even the next morning they could see the sand rippling as the worms circled the crag, as if awaiting their next meal. Perseus was surprised, as it was unusual for the desert worms to hunt their prey for any length of time. They are more opportunistic hunters, often finding prey by accident. This behavior was out of character. He sensed there was some other hand at play in keeping them here, although he did not share his thoughts with the others.

The sun was rising high in the sky, and now the rocks were red hot. They had plenty of water and food, but little protection from the suns harsh rays. They would not be able to stay here much longer, but the worms would not leave.

New tremors began and could be felt under the the ground. For a moment everyone feared that the desert worms were trying to dig through the rocks. The ground around the crag was a maelstrom of whirling sands, and it was obvious that there was much activity going on below the surface.

It was Hendon who resolved the mystery.

"Fear not everyone. I sense that it is the desert worms who are now under attack. They are fleeing from huge, long snakes or lizards. It seems we are being rescued by the Akkedis, and if you thought the desert worms were big, wait until you see these beasts. These are our allies, Perseus, aren't they?" he asked, hopefully.

"The Akkedis are no one's allies. You should never trust them, ever," Perseus warned them. He knew how devious these creatures could be, and while he was grateful for their help, he knew that there would be a price to pay. The Akkedis do not help anyone unless it was for profit.

Gaping holes appeared in the sands, only this time instead of desert worms, giant serpents slithered out of the holes and onto the rocks. Riding on the backs of them rode smaller lizard creatures.

Soon, the Queen's party was completely surrounded by the scaly skinned creatures. Ganry put himself by Myriam's side, hand on sword. He did not draw it just yet as there was no point in antagonizing their rescuers, but he was ready all the same.

Perseus stood at the front of the group and stepped closer to one of the serpents. The rider dismounted and greeted him as he approached. They were in deep discussion as Perseus gesticulated and pointed away at the horizon.

"Do you know what they are saying to each other?" Myriam asked of Hendon.

"Yes, it seems we are to fly away from here on the backs of these creatures. Not only can they burrow through the sands, but they also have wings to take us into the skies."

Perseus and the creature finished their conversation and he came over to update them.

"We will each of us ride on the backs of these winged serpents," he told them as they gathered around him. "We will be accompanied by one of the smaller creatures who will guide us to our destination."

"What about the camels?" Hendon asked. "Are we to leave them at the mercy of the sand worms?"

"The worms have gone. The Akkedis leader tells me that at least four are dead. They have now fled and will be in no hurry to return."

Perseus could see that Hendon was still concerned. Being able to speak to animals gives you an insight and an empathy to their plight.

"Camels are used to roaming this desert, my friend," Perseus assured him. "They know how to make their way home. They will be safe, I promise you."

That seemed to satisfy Hendon and he walked over to the camels and spoke softly to them, as if reassuring them. Perseus followed him, as he also loved the desert beasts.

"Perseus?" Hendon said to him. "They tell me that the lizards kept the sand worms here. Why would they do that if they planned to rescue us?"

"I sensed this was so," Perseus tried to explain. "Never trust the Akkedis. Be wary at all times and stay close to your Queen."

"Why do you continue to travel with us now that we have new guides?" Hendon asked of Perseus, wondering if he, too, could be trusted.

"My master assigned me with this task. I stay until I am of no more use." With that answer he turned to leave the young human male, feeling he had answered enough questions. He did not wish to reveal his real reasons.

Myriam felt apprehensive about flying on the backs of these creatures, but she was happy to be seeing the end of this treacherous desert that had already taken the life of one of their party. How many more lives would be lost in the search for her grandmother?

Perseus's warning about not trusting the Akkedis was fresh in her mind, as was her dream that had shown her grandmother was with the Akkedis, so what choice did they have? At least this way they would reach their destination quickly. She just hoped they weren't rushing into a trap.

They were strapped into saddles on the back of the flying lizards with a guide at their backs, directing the flight. Each sat apprehensively, and a little puzzled at how such cumbersome creatures could take to the air. As if in response to their uncertainty, huge wings were unfurled from their sides, beautiful and almost transparent, filled with intricate patterns in various colors. They glistened like gossamer. The lizards seemed to furl up slightly before suddenly springing forward at speed, until they shot over the end of the rocks with their huge wings beating a rhythm as they soared into the sky.

Myriam loved the experience of flying. She relished the sensation as the winds rushed by her face. Never had she felt so wonderful as she did high in the skies of the world. If only humans could fly, they would travel their journeys so much quicker, and never be attacked by sand worms.

Ganry, on the other hand hated it. He was a man who liked to have his feet firmly planted on the ground. He even hated being on a boat. It was not natural, and if the great maker had wanted them to fly he would have given them wings, he reasoned. He had agreed to strap himself on to this giant monster only because Myriam had insisted. The sooner they were back on the ground the better.

Hendon held up his arms in exhilaration as the winds blew across his face, blowing his hair behind him. He felt like he was experiencing how a bird glided through the skies. Everything below was tiny, even the tallest trees seem to dwarf below them.

Linz felt much like Ganry. This was not where a lake man belonged, and he sat stiffly, gripping his reins as if his life depended on it.

Perseus simply accepted this was a necessary evil. He could not do his duty if he could not enter the city of the Akkedis. He had a task to do and soon all this would be over.

Hendon felt his staff vibrating and then he sensed the old man laughing.

"Do you like flying, Barnaby?" he asked in his mind.

"I love flying," Barnaby chuckled in Hendon's head. "I had heard those blasted worms rumbling the sands around you, but I see you're safe for now, my boy, so I'll be off."

Hendon felt Barnaby leave his mind. Hendon liked Barnaby and wished he'd stay longer as he felt sure that he was an integral part of their mission. He wondered where he went off to when he left him, it did not sound like he stayed upon this world.

Perhaps when you're a spirit you can flit between worlds. As he flew on the back of this creature, with his thoughts on Barnaby, he observed in the distance that there was nothing but sand in every direction.

Yet, the lizards were flying lower as if their journey was coming to an end. He hoped this was not a trick and they were not going to leave them stranded in the desert. He looked over at Perseus who seemed calm and unconcerned, so he decided that all must be well, and as the lizard swooped lower, he awaited the landing with slight trepidation.

CHAPTER 15

In the distance they could see a large oasis on the horizon. This must be their destination, thought Myriam, but it looked far too small to be the Kingdom of the Akkedis. Perhaps they were stopping for water?

The lizards, as they approached the oasis started to circle it, each time getting lower and lower until they were almost brushing the tops of the trees. Then in front of them, an avenue appeared. A long stretch that looked like a straight path cutting through the trees. The lizards swooped down into the gap as they flew lower and lower until they were eventually on the ground.

Everyone dismounted their rides and gathered together. Perseus spoke with the leader and they were told to follow him. He led them between a gathering of tall palm trees and behind them were many large boulders. A passageway appeared between the boulders which seemed to get wider as they walked along it. High upon the boulders, Ganry spotted the look-out guards. His warrior senses warning him of danger, and he would need to be extra vigilant.

"We could not flee now even if we wanted to, Ganry," Myriam said to her bodyguard, seeing his discomfort. "If this is to be a trap then they have lured us in well. All we can do is remain alert. I trust and rely on you Ganry to warn me of any impending danger." She spoke in a quiet voice so only he could hear her words.

He said nothing, but she knew that he had heard her. She too felt uncomfortable in this place.

As the rock walls seemed to get higher, the pathway appeared to be leading in a downwards slope. Soon they entered an entrance to a cave and here the guards were numerous. The air was fast becoming cooler, but there was no damp smell that Myriam would normally associate with caves in her lands. The passageway led into a huge cavern, which gave them the option of many other paths. The underground space was well lit and a hive of activity.

Myriam observed as Ganry approached Perseus, and they were soon in a deep discussion. She was glad Ganry was here. If this was a trap, then he more than anyone else would know how they could make their escape.

A new guide appeared and led them down one of the many openings. Torches burned in sconces, illuminating the dark passages. They seemed to be walking deeper and deeper as the ground beneath them sloped ever downwards. Often they passed other passageways that led off in different directions.

Myriam thought the place must be a huge catacomb, and they would never remember their way out of here without a guide. Finally they arrived on a platform that looked down upon what could only be described as an underground city. As Myriam gazed in astonishment, she could see streets and rooftops, and there was even a market square.

"What an amazing place," Hendon spoke with wonder in his voice. "Who would have thought there could be such a huge city beneath the sands?"

Ganry viewed the city with different eyes. He did not marvel at its wonders, or consider the finer points of how such a city was built. He was a man of action and violence, and they were in a city that held many dangers. His prime focus was on how they could fight their way out, should it become necessary.

Ganry turned to check on Myriam, and from out of the shadows appeared Ghaffar.

"Greetings, Queen Myriam. This is an honor for my people. Never before have we had human royalty as our guests," he said, bowing down to her.

Myriam smiled, almost relieved to have found the little man at last. Ganry however, was much more suspicious at the sudden appearance of the little monk.

"Please come this way. I would like to show you where you will be staying on your visit to our humble city." Ghaffar indicated for them to follow him.

At the bottom of the ramp which led down from the balcony, they were met by a huge lizard that stood on all fours and had short legs, a long snout, and hard knobbly skin. Its long tail swished from side to side. This creature seemed more like a domesticated animal, or a beast of burden, as it had a huge saddle upon its back.

Ghaffar climbed up the saddle and took a seat, indicating for the others to do likewise. A driver sat upon a smaller saddle attached to its broad neck, and he used a whip to direct the lizard.

"Much like using a horse," Ghaffar said to Myriam. "The Ingwenya are our means of transport within the icy. They can even take us under the water. Quite useful, especially in battle. Such a lot of teeth."

Myriam was unsure whether he was joking, or threatening them, but she sensed nothing aggressive in his tone. Glancing around at the others she saw that Linz was staring coldly at Ghaffar. He had been present at the death of his uncle, Chief Clay, and held him responsible for that.

She hoped that if revenge was on his mind, it would wait until they had freed her grandmother. Although she wondered if any of them would manage to ever escape from these caves. How long were the Akkedis going to remain courteous towards them? She wanted to let them believe that they had her where they wanted her, which in reality they probably did, though she did have a few tricks up her sleeves.

Would the power of the stones help them to escape should the Akkedis turn on them? Ganry was a powerful warrior, but even he could not fight an entire Akkedis army. Then there was the elusive Perseus. He had been a good guide, but she couldn't help but feel there was more to him than they knew about. She hoped that they could use that to their benefit should the need arise.

As they moved through the hustle and bustle of an underground city, the air was stifling and the smell was overpowering. Many of the Akkedis stared as they passed them by. They all stood on two legs and dressed in long robes that covered most of their scaly bodies.

All of the Akkedis appeared to be armed. It was most unnerving for Myriam, but she sat upright and showed no sign of fear. Ghaffar seemed to enjoy her discomfort, but she merely smiled at him, showing him nothing but a show of friendship. If this was to be trickery, then she wanted them to make the first move. She would do nothing to antagonize them, but should they show her treachery then she would respond likewise.

"I look forward to seeing my grandmother, Ghaffar. I hope it will be soon?" Myriam smiled at him.

"She has taken a turn for the worse," Ghaffar told her. "Please be patient and you shall see her after you have eaten and rested."

"I was unaware that she was ill," Myriam exclaimed, sitting upright at this dire news.

"Calm yourself, human Queen," Ghaffar almost hissed. "She needs a good night's sleep and all will be well. I have informed her of your coming and she asks for rest before she speaks with you. Is that too much to ask after what she has been through for your Kingdom?"

Myriam did not bother to answer the impertinent little man. If only they could leave this place this very day. If only.

CHAPTER 16

Myriam was given a room of her own. At either side of her, both Linz and Hendon were accommodated. Opposite her room, Ganry and Perseus were given a room together. Ganry was not happy with this arrangement.

With Ghaffar watching on, he made the changes so that the Akkedis were well aware that the Queen was going to be well guarded. He moved Linz and Hendon into the shared room meant for him and Perseus, and at either side of Myriam he put himself and Perseus. He was pleased that Myriam's room had adjoining doors to both her protectors on either side.

"But what about Linz and Hendon? They are alone and unprotected," she said quietly in Ganry's ear.

"They are not unprotected and they are not alone. They have each other, that is enough for them."

As she thought about it, she had to agree it was a better arrangement than Ghaffar had made. She nodded her agreement to Ganry, accepting his lead.

Ghaffar said nothing at this stage even though he was a little annoyed at Ganry's meddling. There was reasoning behind putting the D'Anjue bloodline in the adjoining rooms, but it mattered little. Soon this farce would be over and the pretense done away with.

Of course, he could simply take them all prisoner right here and now, but that would affect the quality of the blood. He needed the three D'Anjue family members to remain calm.

Fear and stress created a chemical reaction in the blood, affecting its quality. Ghaffar simply smiled as the party of humans rearranged themselves. No matter, he could still carry out his duties, and maybe the two male D'Anjue bloodlines would be easier targets housed together.

"I trust you would like to clean up after your long journey. We will meet for dinner, is this acceptable?" Ghaffar asked.

Myriam accepted the invitation to dine. Ghaffar smiled and bid them goodbye, for now.

Once he had gone, Ganry entered Myriam's room and checked it was secure. He checked the windows and the walls for secret passages.

Myriam looked longingly at the bath of hot soapy water in her room as Ganry carried out his checking of her room. Eventually he seemed satisfied, and using the adjoining door he entered his own room and left her alone.

She quickly stripped and was soon soaking in the hot water. What a luxury. Finally getting to wash some of that sand from her hair and the grime from her skin. She lay there a while, luxuriating on the suds, before she climbed out of the bath, dried herself, and lay on her soft bed to relax.

It seemed that Ghaffar had thought of everything. She slipped into a loose robe that was provided, similar to the ones she had seen the women in these lands wear.

Bathtubs of hot water was set up in all the rooms for the travelers, but only one in the shared room. Linz and Hendon argued over who would go first.

"Pah, I am a Chief of my people, and you are simply a forest dweller!" Linz argued good-naturedly before promptly stripping off his clothing and jumping into the warm tub, splashing half the water all over the floor.

"If the sand at the bottom of that bath scratches at my backside, then I will boil the Chief of the lake people in the waters he bathes in," Hendon threatened.

He was not really bothered about being last in the water. He was just so relieved to be out of the dreaded desert. Hendon went to lay on his bed, still fully clothed in his dirty traveling garments. He hoped he would not fall asleep before Linz was finished, or that the water was not freezing cold by his turn. They really should have put two tubs in this room.

Ganry bathed in his tub and welcomed the hot soapy water on his weary body. Despite the pleasure the bath gave him, Ganry was quickly out and dressed in the fresh clothes the Akkedis had provided. He put on his cloak before setting out to check on the others.

His first call was to Hendon and Linz. He saw that Linz had already bathed, but Hendon looked like he'd fallen asleep in the tub, so he kicked the side, startling Hendon awake.

"Never be unawares of your surroundings, boy!" Ganry growled at him. "Not unless you wish to lose your head."

Ganry followed Linz out of the open doorway, leaving a stunned Hendon in a cold bathtub.

Soon, with everyone bathed and rested, they all gathered in Myriam's room as Ganry had instructed so he could speak to them.

"I have a bad feeling about this place. All is not what it seems and it is important that we do not get separated." He paused, looking at each of them. "At night, we will have a rotation of guards. This night I will take first watch. Hendon, you can be next, seeing as you've already slept."

Hendon smiled ruefully as he remembered his rude awakening in the freezing cold bathtub. Had Ganry not woken him up he would have frozen to death.

Before Ganry could continue there was a knock at the door and a female Akkedis entered. She was a slender shape and walked on her hind legs with no apparent difficulty. This had been bred into the Akkedis over many centuries. Myriam thought her eyes looked friendly and she attempted to speak with her.

"My name is Myriam, what shall I call you?' she asked her, only to receive a hiss of the creatures long, forked tongue.

Myriam spoke no more and followed the female as she had indicated for them to do so, leading them through an array of passageways.

"Keep trying to befriend any that you can," Ganry whispered quietly in her ear. "We will be in need of allies, sooner or later."

She smiled back at him. Was he setting her mind at ease or did he just give her an order? Still, he was right, not all the Akkedis would be hostile. Some may be sympathetic to their cause and willing to help once they were facing real danger.

Ganry noticed that Perseus lagged at the back of the group. He was happy to give him this position as he could concentrate on what was to come in the front. Hendon was busy muttering to his staff but Linz, at least, seemed alert.

They arrived in a large oval room and in the center stood a huge table, ladened with food of all varieties. Various meats, spiced vegetables and colorful fruits, were laid out for them. Myriam felt unsure and stopped in her tracks. Linz approached her, wondering what worried her so.

"Myriam, what ails you?" he asked.

"How do we know that none of this contains poison?"

Hendon stood behind them and tapped Linz on the shoulder with his staff. Linz moved aside to allow Hendon into the conversation.

"I have been speaking with Barnaby on such matters and he assures me all is well. He has looked into the food and there are no traces of anything harmful."

Linz was the first to sit down and eat, and the others soon followed. Even Perseus joined them and ate his fill. He knew he needed some newly stored energy, ahead of the battle to come.

CHAPTER 17

The same female Akkedis returned after they had eaten and took them all back to their chambers. Once she had gone, they all gathered in Ganry's room, with the exception of Perseus who was acting rather strange. Ganry had caught him in his room, appearing in a trance. He had just assumed he was praying to which-ever god he believed in.

"You must thank the spirit of Barnaby for assuring us about the food." Myriam's voice broke Ganry's thought. "We would have all gone to bed hungry if it were not for him," she said to Hendon.

"Actually, I'm beginning to think he's more than a spirit, Myriam. I suspect he is from another dimension or world. When we talk, it's as if he's still alive, but somewhere else."

"How strange." Myriam thought about what Hendon had said, but it was too fantastical for her to compre-hend.

"Why do you suppose we have not seen my grand-mother yet?" she asked, changing the subject to something more earthly.

"I'm not sure," Ganry replied, "but I feel there is something going on here that we know nothing of. They are keeping something from us."

"You don't think my grandmother to be dead, do you?" she dared to ask him.

"If she were, I believe we would sense it," Linz answered, recalling the strength of the stones and the magic within the D'Anjue bloodline. "I do feel a weariness in this place, but I suppose it's the lack of fresh air to breath in. The air within the Cefinon Forest is humid, but this place is far worse," Linz complained.

"Living underground does not seem natural to me," Hendon agreed. "I'm sure these creatures need air as much as we do, but they don't seem to mind if it's not fresh. I would miss the skies and the rivers. I do hope we're not down here too long."

"I would leave now if we could, dear Hendon," Myriam said, also uneasy with being deep underground.

"Being down here is as natural as being on the surface. It's just meant for different creatures. We are surface creatures and the Akkedis are more at home under the earth." Ganry joined in the conversation. "Perseus and I will be going for a walk around the immediate corridors. I would like to map out this place a little, get some bearing of where we are."

"I'm afraid we cannot allow that," a voice said from the opening doorway.

Ghaffar walked in, leaving a couple of guards outside the door.

"I trust you are much refreshed now that you have bathed and eaten?" he inquired, as if they were here on pleasurable business.

The Queen nodded her affirmation. "Yes Ghaffar, thank you for your hospitality. I hope that my visit will help bring our two nations together in a closer union."

Ganry smiled to himself. The young Queen was quickly becoming the wise diplomat.

"Now we are rested I had hoped we could see my grandmother, before I retire." Myriam emphasized this point to Ghaffar. "I am concerned for her and will not rest easy until I see her."

"Of course, Queen Myriam." Ghaffar bowed in an exaggerated manner. "That is the purpose of my visit this evening, to take you to see your grandmother."

Ganry stood up and walked up to the small frame of Ghaffar's human looking body. He towered over him but the little man showed no signs of being intimidated by Ganry's muscular physique.

"I will accompany the Queen to see her grandmother," he informed him, making it clear this was not a request. "The Queen goes nowhere alone."

"You are not in a position to make such demands, Ganry the brave. She will not be alone, I will be with her." Ghaffar sneered at the big human, his address to Ganry, mocking him. Still, Ghaffar did not want to antagonize them just yet. "Very well, you may come along, but you cannot map our corridors. Remember, you are a guest here, and guests act with respect in the homes that they visit. This is the way of humans, is it not?"

"Truly," Myriam responded on behalf of Ganry before he could speak. "We have every respect for your community. I am truly grateful for the care you have provided to my grandmother. However, we wish for her to return to her own home as soon as possible."

"Of course, and I shall facilitate that in any way I can, Queen Myriam, when she is well." Ghaffar bowed again. "For now she is bed ridden, and I am taking the greatest of care for her well being. A woman of the Duchess' standing, deserves nothing but the best treatment that we can provide."

Myriam seated herself in a chair, a little shocked at this news.

"Are you saying my grandmother is very ill? I thought it just a part of her recovery from the dungeon, not an illness?"

"Please, Queen Myriam, let us go along and visit her," Ghaffar suggested, as he opened the door and gestured for them to follow him.

Myriam looked over at Ganry who nodded, indicating that she should go first. Myriam followed Ghaffar out of the door, and Ganry followed his Queen. They walked in procession down an array of corridors cut into the rock, dimly lit by the torches on the walls.

Ganry tried to memorize the way, but he suspected that they were being led in an indirect route. In fact, he was certain that they had been on this current corridor at least once already today, but he could never be certain in this confounded place. If the route taken was meant to confuse them then it had done its task well.

Finally, Ghaffar turned into a doorway and stepped into a dimly lit room. The entourage followed him in and there Myriam saw her grandmother, lain in bed and unresponsive. Quickly going to her side, she knelt on the floor and took a hold of her grandmother's hand. It felt cold and clammy to touch, and Myriam feared the worse.

"Do you know what ails her?" she asked of Ghaffar, almost accusingly.

"She suffered much at the hands of the pretender, Harald, and endured much in the dungeons of the castle. I rescued her from there, as soon as I could, but now you see the consequences of that terrible experience," he explained.

Myriam knew there was truth in the tale. Her grandmother had suffered much physical and mental pain to save her throne. This was her fault, not the Akkedis. As Ghaffar had pointed out, he had been the one to rescue her. She had much to thank him for.

The Duchess appeared unaware of anything happening around her, looking pale and almost lifeless. Her skin was cold, but she did still live. Her heart was still beating, just.

"I can only thank you, Ghaffar, you and your people, for all that you have done for my family. Finding my grandmother is a joyous occasion for my heart. I am just saddened to see her this way. I had hoped to travel home immediately, but I can see now that my grandmother is in no state to be journeying across the desert. We must burden you longer and hope that now I am by her side, that she may begin to recover."

Ghaffar merely bowed his head, saying nothing. His plan had worked well by letting the Duchess slip into unconsciousness. It had served to keep the D'Anjue family here longer, without having to use any kind of force to do so. His Empress would be pleased with his results and would reward him richly.

CHAPTER 18

Artas knew that ruling in Myriam's absence would be difficult, but he did not realize just how difficult a task it would prove to be. He had hoped to keep a low profile until the Queen returned, but the politicians and merchants were making his life a misery. Their demands to have a private audience with the Queen was a daily occurrence, one he was finding more difficult every day to keep them at bay. Soon they would guess the truth, that Myriam was no longer here, and when they did he was not sure how it would end.

And now to make matters worse, a distant relative of Myriam's, Lord Josiah, had arrived at the castle with a small private army demanding to see the Queen.

"Should I rouse the soldiers and ride out to meet this Lord?" Artas asked his close advisors, Parsival and Leonie. "I would prefer to battle a hundred dragons than have to face these greedy, conniving individuals," he declared, totally and utterly defeated.

"Our main concern is not the traders or politicians within the city, it is those who make greater demands of the throne," Parsival explained. "Josiah is a distant relative of Myriam's, on her father's side, and he feels he has claim to lands in this kingdom. And maybe he does, as his lands were lost under the Usurper. If we show weakness now then we will be inundated with distant relatives from all over the lands laying their claims. Only Josiah is aware of the Queen's departure from her kingdom. True, he does have a small army that will cause this town a hardship, but my friend, we need only use delaying tactics on such a toad."

"The people will soon learn that the Queen does not reside in her castle, that is inevitable," Leonie said her part. "This is where you need to use your influence, honorary or otherwise. Call in your chiefs, their Queen needs them. Be decisive, Artas, tell these people, don't ask them."

The Duchess felt herself floating. The blood in her veins was working so hard, it had become depleted and what remained was attempting to keep her heart pumping. Her heart struggled, something evil was infiltrating her veins and taking away the very magic that had kept her healthy for so long in her life. It was not the magic within her blood that failed her, it was more that something was taking the magic out of her very veins.

She had felt the presence of her granddaughter, imaginary or real, she could not tell. Whatever it was, she had tried to reach out to her but she simply did not have the strength to awaken from the deep sleep that had taken over her body.

Myriam, Myriam, I am here. Wake me up if you can for I am still here, she called out in her dreams.

Were they dreams or was she simply dead? She felt no pain, only a need to rest. This shell of a body could function no more. She would have to let it go soon. It was such hard work holding on. She longed for the light of the sun. Why couldn't she find it?

Her granddaughter's presence faded and she was once again alone. Then the pain started up again, a drumming noise in her ear, like a pump pounding within her veins. A stinging sensation shivered through her entire body and her muscles seized up tightly as she convulsed on the bed.

The female Akkedis, known by her friends as Arriba, felt sorry for the dying woman. She had seemed such a kindly human. As she replaced the pump back into the woman's veins, she wondered at how much more this frail human frame could take. The Akkedis Empress was demanding more in her drink or she too could die. This human was her lifeline and she worried that the woman did not have much more liquid left to give. If the Empress was to live, then Ghaffar needed to act quickly, or their world would be in chaos.

Myriam was heartbroken at what she had witnessed. She wanted to demand that her grandmother be put in her room, but Ganry had cautioned against this, for now. Why was Ganry advising this? She needed to care for her grandmother, and right now she cared little for anything else.

"Ganry, we have traveled long and hard to find the Duchess. I do not believe my grandmother will be in this world for much longer and yet you tell me not to make demands. Why?" Myriam had always trusted Ganry's judgment because he had always put her life before his own, yet this did not make any sense.

"Myriam," he called her by her first name, "I know the Duchess suffers greatly, but I do not believe she is ill. I think there is more to her condition than the injuries caused by Duke Harald. I fear for your life, and as Queen, I must beg you not to put yourself in danger until we can avoid it no more."

"You believe that the Akkedis are killing my grandmother?" Myriam was unsure if this was what Ganry was implying. Surely not? Ghaffar had rescued the Duchess from the pits of hell within the dungeons of the castle. Then he had got her far away from the dangers. Didn't that make him her savior?

"I too feel that we are all in danger in this city," Linz offered his advise. "There is something linking the legend of the Rooggaru and Ghaffar, but I have not managed to unravel the mystery. He appeared as a monk in the temple on many occasions, and he was there the night that my uncle was killed. I am wary of him and think he means us harm."

CHAPTER 19

Ganry decided it was time to approach Perseus and see what his part was to be in all of this. If he had a battle on his hands then he would need Perseus at his side, but he was not sure if he could be trusted.

When he entered Perseus's room it was empty, with no sign of him anywhere. He had many questions for this elusive Vandemlander, and so took a seat in a chair by the door and waited for Perseus to return. He wondered where he could have gone. None of them were allowed to wander unhindered through the caves. He hoped that he had not come to any harm. He would need his blade if they needed to fight their way out.

A movement on the floor caught his attention and he quickly stood, drawing his sword. A snake, long with a thick body and a scaly skin of many colors writhed out from under the bed. He must have missed it when he entered the room. Had it eaten Perseus? No. He doubted that a warrior of Perseus's ability would be overcome by a snake, even one as huge as this one.

The snake quickly moved towards Ganry, its tongue slithering in and out of a wide mouth, making hissing noises. Its upper body raised up high, standing upright. The bottom half of its scaled body lay pooled in a circle on the floor.

Its red eyes stared into Ganry's, as if searching for his soul. The weak could easily become mesmerized by those hypnotic eyes. Ganry lowered his sword, Windstorm, holding it at his side. This ancient piece of weaponry had been forged by Grimlock bladesmiths in the Limestone Mountains. Few would survive its sharp edge, not even the thick scales of a giant snake. Yet he sensed this beast would do him no harm.

What occurred next caused Ganry to doubt his own eyes as he witnessed the snake transforming into Perseus, who bowed his head, his palms together in a greeting.

"I am able to slip and slide within the walls, Ganry, and find out much needed information. I am almost ready to complete my task for my master, Qutaybah."

Ganry slid Windstorm back into its scabbard and he sat back down in the chair, wondering at what Perseus was really about.

"Something tells me that your mission here was not just to deliver our Queen to her grandmother, am I right, Perseus?" Ganry asked.

The door to the outside corridor opened and Ghaffar stood there. At first he looked annoyed and said nothing. Was he aware of Perseus's trips within the walls?

"Empress Gishja has requested an audience with Queen Myriam. You are all to attend," he said curtly, closing the door behind him as he left.

"It seems we are summoned, Perseus. I hope it is nothing to do with your tour of the caves," Ganry said as he knocked on the adjoining door that led to Myriam's room.

As he opened it, he saw that Myriam was resting on her bed. Her yellow blonde hair was loose upon her pillow and she looked truly beautiful. Fleetingly, he was reminded of his own of daughter, Ruby, who would have been around the same age as the Queen.

In those dark days after he had lost his wife and daughter, he had cared little for his own life and he had served as a mercenary, taking the most dangerous of commissions. But serving Myriam had given him a reason to live again, and he would serve her until his death. He placed his hand on her shoulder and shook her gently.

"My Queen, we have been summoned by the Akkedis Empress. Would you like to freshen up?"

Myriam sat up and rubbed her eyes. Her sleep on an evening was restless and she often found herself drifting off to sleep during the day, if it was indeed daytime. Who knew so deep underground.

"Gather the others, Ganry, I will ready myself," she said, automatically seeking out the dagger, Harkan, that she kept under her pillow. Whenever she held it in the hand with the matching ring, it would shine with a white light and then fade out again, almost as if it had charged itself ready for battle.

She pulled at the necklace that Barnaby had given her. Recently it had felt heavy around her neck and had rubbed at her skin. She looked in the mirror, her hand going to a red mark just under her jawline. It was around two inches long and seemed to rise in an inflamed mound, at its center a puncture mark. How had that got there?

When Barnaby gave her the necklace, he said it had magical properties and would ward off anything harmful, but so far it had done nothing, though it was very pretty. Now that she looked upon it, she recalled a dream she had of the necklace. It had been trying to awaken her because she was choking, but yet she could not awaken. She seemed to be having many strange dreams in this place, dreams that disturbed her, making her sleep fitful.

Linz and Hendon entered her room. She looked at Hendon as he also had an identical necklace, but she could not see it.

"Where is the necklace given to you by Barnaby?" she asked, concerned that he really needed to be wearing it.

"I gave it to Linz because I have the staff now, a direct link with Barnaby who protects me at all times," he told her.

She looked at Linz and noticed the necklace around his darker skinned neck.

"How are you two sleeping?" she asked of them.

"If you mean does Linz snore loud enough to keep me awake so I cannot sleep, then no I'm not sleeping well," Hendon replied.

Linz laughed. "I sleep very well, Myriam. As for Hendon, he's too busy mumbling to his staff, but I simply shut out his noise and I'm soon in a peaceful slumber."

"I only ask because I think my necklace is active when I sleep. It awakens me with some sort of warning. Do you think it has caused these marks?" She showed them the single puncture wound on her throat.

"The Empress is not pleased, Arriba. Why were you unable to draw blood from the female?" Ghaffar questioned one of his servants. "Have you lost your touch of invisibility?"

"No, Ghaffar, I have not. My magic remains in my blood for ever and I will continue to serve the Empress always. The girl wears a necklace and when I punctured her skin to take her juices, the necklace burned me. I then tried to puncture elsewhere on her body, but the necklace kept attacking me with burns. When I grabbed it to try and pull it from her neck, it awoke her, so I had to leave."

"A necklace?" Ghaffar had not heard of such a thing. "I know of the stones, but these are of Akkedis origin, so we should be able to control their magic. I know nothing of any necklace. We must try to steal this thing away."

CHAPTER 20

A female Akkedis came to take them to the meeting with their Empress, but first they were all led to a chamber with many heated baths. It seemed a custom to bathe before an audience with the Empress. The cavern smelled strongly of sulphur. Guards stood around one empty bath, but the others contained many Akkedis, washing themselves.

"This place stinks." Hendon was first to speak, though he said it quietly. It would not do to upset all the Akkedis that surrounded them.

"I will explain to them our etiquette with regards to human bathing," Ganry said to Myriam. "It seems that the Akkedis do not differentiate their females from the males. I will see if I can obtain a private bathing area for you."

"No, Ganry," Myriam stopped him. "I feel this a test of my resolve. Let us make the most of this hot, bubbling water and bathe together. We are all friends, and I am sure you will divert your eyes at the appropriate moments." She smiled at Ganry for his thoughtfulness.

The hot spa was refreshing on her naked skin and she felt cleaned. If this was some ploy by Ghaffar, then it had backfired on him. It seemed the little man was becoming more daring. It would only be a matter of time before they would be treated as prisoners and no longer guests. She took her time in the hot spa to think on her present situation. Soon, it would be time to act and make their escape, but could they take the Duchess with them?

"Your Queen and all of you are in danger," Perseus informed Ganry as they bathed in the hot pool.

"I knew that the minute we set off." Ganry was not surprised at Perseus's words of warning. "What I do not know is what your part is in this, Perseus, because I do not believe it to be that of a guide."

"I am sworn to protect your Queen and the Duchess, and I am not your enemy, Ganry, of that you can be certain. But I fear it may be too late for the Duchess." Perseus did not wish to explain his role. What these human's did not know, they could not repeat. It was better that way.

"Do you know what ails the Duchess?"

Perseus knew very well what ailed the Duchess, but could not divulge this information for fear of jeopardizing his own plans.

"We should ask the Lizard Empress if the Duchess can be moved to her granddaughter's room. She no longer serves a purpose for the Akkedis in her present state, so I think she will agree to this," Perseus said. He knew they had almost drained the Duchess dry of her blood juices, and she was very close to death. "Convince the Akkedis Empress that if the Duchess rests with those who she loves, she will make a full recovery and will soon be fit again. This will please the Empress."

He knew that this would build up her blood supply once again, but the Akkedis seemed unaware that all they needed to do was let the patient rest in between sessions. If he could get them to convey this message to the Akkedis, it may buy the Duchess some time.

"Whatever do you mean, Perseus?" Myriam had been slowly moving over towards the men, hiding her modesty beneath the water. "Are you saying that my grandmother was serving some sort of purpose for the Akkedis?" Myriam was confused at his words.

"Blood!" Linz whispered as he waded through the water in their direction. "The Rooggaru fed from my uncle's blood. That is how the Akkedis feed."

"Are you saying that Ghaffar is taking my grandmother's blood?" Myriam gasped.

"That puts us all in danger then. We've all got a good supply," Hendon said as he also moved closer to the group.

Ganry pointed out the obvious. "In case you have not already noticed, my dear Hendon, we are already in danger and have been ever since we came to this city."

"That's what I dreamed about, I remember now," Myriam recalled. "My necklace stopped them from taking my blood, that's why it burned at my skin, to warn me."

"You mean they were in your room?" Ganry was angry with the Akkedis, but more angry with himself as he had checked that room for secret passages. "They did not enter through the door, so there must be another way into your chamber. Tonight, we swap rooms. I'll be interested to see who's paying you a visit in your sleep."

The female Akkedis, Arriba, appeared at the edge of the pool. She again was allocated to the humans.

"It is time," she said to them. "The Empress is ready to receive you." She bowed her head.

"Listen," Ganry addressed the group. "We most not let them know we are aware of this. We are not yet ready to face them down."

Despite his calm words, Ganry was furious with the Akkedis, angry that they had kidnapped the Duchess, but even more angry that they threatened Myriam. He may be urging caution now, but one day in the not too distant future, these lizards would pay a heavy price for their treachery, and Ganry would personally see to it.

They all nodded their agreement before leaving the baths.

None of the menfolk seemed to be aware that they had climbed from the pool naked, but Myriam stayed in the water. Whilst she had managed to get into the pool, she was now suddenly self conscious of her nakedness. Linz approached the edge of the water with a towel, grateful that these creatures used such things.

"It seems the Akkedis Empress wants us cleaned up before she eats us for dinner," Linz joked.

Myriam could not see the funny side of his jest. It was just a little too close to the truth.

CHAPTER 21

The Queen's party were led into a new area of the caves, one that they had not seen before. Though it was hard to tell one stone passageway from another, this new area was better lit and had fresher air to breath.

Led into a huge chamber, they all stared in wonder at the glittering walls of crystals. Many rare stones came from these regions so it was not a surprise to see them, but the wall was covered in a shimmering glow of twinkling rainbow colors. It was magnificent.

The tall vaulted ceiling rose so high above them that they could not see where the walls ended. In the center of the chamber on a raised bejeweled dais, sat the Akkedis ruler, Empress Gishja, overlooking her subjects.

This truly was a royal chamber, Myriam thought, and the Empress was a frightening sight for any human. Her scaled body shone with an almost luminous green. The form of her body was eerily human shaped, only more that of a bent old person with a permanently misshaped backbone. The lumpy bone was clearly visible through her thick scaled skin before it merged into a thick, long snake-like tail.

Her feet and hands were adorned with long sharp claws. But it was the face that unnerved Myriam the most. It looked cruel and unfriendly, with wide yellow eyes that never seemed to blink. Her head had high protruding cheekbones adorned with wiry hair, plaited into straight vertical lines. The little pointed chin mimicked a human face, a cruel face, one that had never shown any mercy.

Ghaffar appeared at the side of his Empress and spoke to the new arrivals. "Empress Gishja welcomes the humans into her city, and hopes that they will repay her kindness of saving the human Duchess. What do you offer our Empress for such generosity?" he asked, directing his look at Myriam.

"I cannot know what riches the great Empress Gishja is in need of," Myriam replied. "If my grandmother is allowed to come and share my chamber, where I can care for her, she will soon recover fully and we will not burden the Akkedis Empress with our presence much longer. When I return to my Kingdom, I can send forth any payment the Empress would consider suitable."

"What if the payment I require is more than you can afford, human Queen?" Gishja hissed.

"You cannot know this until you name your price, Empress Gishja." Myriam would show no fear, as this she had been well trained for. "I value my grandmother dearly and I am willing to reward you richly for your help in caring for her and keeping her safe."

"I need no riches, human girl." Gishja spoke with the hiss of a snake, if a snake could speak.

"Then let us burden you no longer and be off on our way," Myriam suggested.

"You take my hospitality and run, what sort of a gratitude is that?"

"I will send you a hundred horses so your people may roam the desert lands with comfort." Myriam stood her ground, staring the Akkedis Empress right into her yellow mesmerizing eyes.

"We have no need of such creatures. We do not eat that which you call meat," Gishja replied, almost laughing.

"What is it that Empress Gishja requires from the human lands as a reward for her kindness?" Myriam asked.

"I require blood," Gishja spat out loudly, showing a long forked, black-red tongue. "Can you supply me with this?"

"Indeed I can, Empress Gishja. We have an abundance of livestock in our lands. There are many full bred cattle, pigs and sheep. If this is important to your people, then yes, I can supply such creatures that will give you such sustenance."

"You insult me, human. Animal blood is not the requirement of Akkedis royalty!" Gishja filled the room with her anger, her voice echoing around the vast chamber.

All was silent, not even a breath could be heard.

"Royalty requires royal blood, human, can you fill my cup with that?"

Myriam knew what was coming, but it still rocked her to her very core. They were in desperate danger now, and she was left in no doubt that the Empress was threatening her very life. The time had come. They were no longer guests, but prisoners of the Akkedis people.

"No!" Myriam shouted out for all to hear. "I cannot provide such a price. I can feed your people, as I have promised, but I cannot fulfill your personal requirements, Empress Gishja."

Myriam had hoped that some of those who would overhear her would be sympathetic to their plight. There must be many Akkedis who were unhappy being ruled by such a treacherous Empress. A union between the two people would have many advantages for both their nations, and she was certain that some here would see the benefit in that. Yet, this Empress was blatantly making the human's her enemy.

"Then you do not value the life of your grandmother very well, do you, human?" Gishja's voice filled the chamber once again. "Guards, take them all prisoner. Keep them together, it will make my feasting so much easier," the Akkedis Empress instructed, no longer willing to keep up the charade of the welcoming host.

"So much for rescuing the Duchess, Ghaffar, only to murder her entire family," Ganry cried out above the noise of the approaching guards. "I salute you for your trickery. I look forward to removing your head from your shoulders in repayment."

Ghaffar bowed low to him. He had done well and his Empress would reward him greatly. Soon she would be healthy again with her new supply of D'Anjue blood flowing into her cup.

CHAPTER 22

Ganry's anger rose as he stared at the slimy Ghaffar. He drew his sword swept it in a wide arc to keep the guards at bay. Perseus had mirrored his actions on the other side of their small circle, Myriam and the others shielded between the two veteran warriors.

Ganry looked around and witnessed more Akkedis guards heading in their direction at speed.

"How many do you think we could kill, Perseus, before we are overcome? I believe I could take at least a score, maybe more."

"Between us, double that," Perseus laughed.

"Let's make the Akkedis regret the day they double crossed us."

In between swings of his sword, Ganry saw the Akkedis Empress was being led out of the chamber surrounded by her royal guards. Ghaffar though, did not warrant such protection and Ganry managed to throw a small dagger that grazed Ghaffar's cheek, causing blood to flow, before embedding in the wall behind him.

"Hah!" Ganry chortled. "Next time if will be your throat, little creature."

"Filthy Palarian!" Ghaffar shouted at him. "You will pay for this, dearly."

"I want them alive," the Lizard Empress instructed as she was hurriedly pushed through the door and out of the chamber.

Ghaffar quickly followed her, his hand over the wound on his cheek, cursing the human as he fled. That fool would regret the day that he had marked him. He would personally make him suffer, Ghaffar promised to himself. By the time he had finished with him, he will have wished he had died here today.

With the Akkedis Empress and Ghaffar gone, Ganry turned his attention to the lizard creatures that were surrounding them. Myriam seemed in no immediate danger. She stood tall and proud, her face impassive. If they were to ever get out of this alive, she would make a wonderful Queen of Palara.

"Well my friend," Perseus said, "shall we do battle? Make them pay for their treachery?"

With those words he leapt high into the air, sword drawn before landing between two large lizards and embedding it into the throat of one of them, before he quickly spun on the balls of his feet and removed the head from the shoulders of the other.

"The skin is tough, Perseus, but it holds little resistance to a sharp blade," Ganry cried, his sword hacking and slashing at their tough skins.

Ganry found himself facing three guards, their swords extended in front of them as they cautiously tried to engage him, wary of his weapon. They had seen a number of their colleagues fall and were in no rush to join them.

Suddenly one of them raised the courage to attack, and lunged at Ganry with a cry of victory in its throat. This soon turned into a death rattle as Ganry's sword speared through its neck, the fabled blade slipping through the scales before protruding out of its back. The creature fell to the floor in a crumple, its blood staining the sandy ground of the royal chamber.

One of the remaining lizards spun around quickly, its tail whipping against Ganry's legs sending him tumbling to the ground. Two Akkedis lizards were soon on him, pinning him to the floor.

Ganry managed to raise another of his daggers and plunge it into one of the lizard's ear, pressing it all the way in until the hilt stopped it from going any deeper. The creature screamed out its agony, with hot, sticky blood gushing out onto Ganry as it slumped dead on top of him. Before he could kill the other, more lizards were on him, pinning his arms to the ground. Looking across to his right, he could see that Perseus was in the same situation. He too was pinned down by a number of the Akkedis guards.

Breathless, Ganry had no regrets that he had chosen to attack the enemy. They needed to know that they would not give up without a fight. He worried for Myriam and the plans these scaly creatures had for her. Right now, he was powerless to help her.

"It was good to have you by my side, Ganry," Perseus said to him as they lay trapped beneath the heavy Akkedis that held them down.

He nodded his acknowledgment. Ganry relaxed and stopped struggling under the weight of the Akkedis who practically sat on top of him. They were soon dragged to their feet.

Ganry smiled at Perseus who had also been pulled up. He looked a mess, and Ganry was certain that he must look the same, clothing disheveled and torn, blood, most of it their enemies, covering them. He had some satisfaction knowing that some Akkedis had paid part of the price for their treachery.

Dragged from the chamber, they were led into a procession of tunnels. Every now and then one of the Akkedis guards would strike them with their heavy scaled fists. They had been instructed not to kill them, but it was clear that they were determined to make them suffer for the colleagues they had lost in the chamber. By the time they reached the dungeons, both were bruised and bloody from the blows.

With hands and feet chained together, they were strapped to the walls, the chains pulling tight so that their feet only just touched the ground. As they hung there, a female Akkedis approached them with a bucket before throwing freezing cold water all over them.

Ganry cried out at the shock of the water on his bruised body.

"You do well to remain quiet, human," the female said to him.

He looked at her. She was familiar, and he realized she had served them in the rooms.

"You do well, Arriba, to stay away, in case I get loose," he answered her back with viciousness.

She hissed and walked out of the chamber, leaving the two males hanging in their chains.

CHAPTER 23

"Do not treat me like a fool, boy," Lord Josiah spat. He was so close to Artas that spittle showered his face. "I demand to see the Queen, and we all know that you cannot meet such a request because she has abandoned her people, is that not so, sir?"

Artas remained calm. He too had a noble upbringing and followed the etiquette that any situation dictated. This one was forcing him to remain civilized in the face of revolt.

"Our Queen is on a mission to save this Kingdom, Lord Josiah. That does not mean that the Kingdom is in jeopardy. Indeed, Queen Myriam is busy making this Kingdom stronger." Artas would not divulge the whole tale, not to this minor royal from the outlands.

Stood in the middle of open ground on the outskirts of the castle was not an ideal place to have such a discussion. Many townsfolk were gathering to witness the confrontation. Rumor had spread that there was to be another coup, and this was not news the citizens of Palara wanted to hear.

"You say she is on some dangerous mission, yet she does not take her army," the Duke spat back. "Putting herself in danger. For all we know she may be dead already and the throne stands vacant." He pauses for his words to take effect with the surrounding throng of people. If they thought she was dead, then they would be more accepting to a member of her family, such as him, taking up the crown. "So it is good that I am here, on hand, to take over the throne while she is absent. I will be Regent until she returns."

"That will not be necessary," Lord Parsival interrupted his fellow Lord as he stood by the side of Artas. "We have a Regent, and I suggest you bow down to him, Lord Josiah. He was put in place by our own Queen, through all the official channels. You, sir, would simply be another usurper and this Kingdom has had its fare share of them." Parsival did not intend on allowing this arrogant Lord to overthrow their present Regent.

"How can this foolish boy be the Kingdom's Regent? He does not even carry one drop of royal blood within his veins. This is an absolute insult to the people of this Kingdom. I will take charge immediately, and any who stand in my way will suffer my wrath," Lord Josiah threatened.

Lady Leonie now joined in the affray. "Sir, we have documentation to support Regent Artas Holstein, who's family have served the royal bloodline for many years. Indeed, they died with the King. They have earned this badge. Our Queen would not have chosen him had she not trusted him."

"For all we know these papers could be falsified," the Lord intimated. "You three could have killed our Queen and taken the power of her seat for yourselves." He gripped his sword hilt and took a menacing step closer towards them. It was obvious that the minor lord was looking for a fight, and Artas would either have to back down, or call his bluff.

"This has gone far enough, Lord Josiah," Artas finally retaliated. "I am placing you under arrest as a threat to the throne. You will remain imprisoned within the castle walls until the return of Queen Myriam, who can then decide your fate."

With that, a very red faced Lord Josiah huffed in indignation, his eyes bulging. He drew his sword from its scabbard, pointing it threateningly at Artas.

"How dare you threaten me, you fool? My armies will overrun this place in an instant. It will be you, sir, who will languish in the dungeons." Turning to his men, he rallied them to his aid. "Take your up your arms. We are overrunning the castle. Kill all of those who stand in your way!" he yelled at his men.

Lord Josiah's men were unsure exactly what they were being ordered to do. There were not enough of them in number to overrun a castle. They were a simple traveling bodyguard, and the castle would be very well defended by a much larger army. Still, if their Lord ordered such action, they were obliged to comply. As one, they all drew their arms and confronted the castle guards.

The gathered citizens gasped at the turn of events. Soldiers confronting the castle defenders and all readying to engage in combat. They had only just recovered from the last coup, one that had caused much hardship and loss of life, and they certainly did not want another usurper ruling them.

Later, when discussing that day in the bars and taverns of the castle, no-one could be certain who made the first move, who had made that rallying cry. But as one they had all taken up arms to protect their castle from the offending soldiers. Armed with pitchforks and scythes, they stood side by side with the castle guards, in solidarity.

Artas looked upon the people in amazement, though his army far outnumbered Lord Josiah's he was grateful that Myriam had the support of her citizens. All they needed now was the return of their Queen.

"I suggest you lay down your arms, Lord Josiah. The people of the Kingdom have spoken. You will not rule here in the Queen's absence." Artas spread his arms, emphasizing the actions of the citizens.

The Duke had not noticed that the townsfolk were threatening his own small force. All he was interested in was getting into the throne room and taking charge of the seat of power. He looked around and for the first time he realized the numbers of the castle's army. Some had remained hidden behind the huge castle gates, but now they marched forward, surrounding his own men.

Plus the imbeciles of this town thought they could threaten him with their meager tools. This was an outrage, and absolute insult to his family. For now he would concede, as he had no choice, but he promised to himself that this was not to be the end of his rebellion. He would demand to be treated as was fitting of his bloodline.

"And what do you intend on doing with me and my men?" he demanded to know.

"I have a room awaiting your arrival," Artas informed him. "Your men will be sent marching to your own lands. You sir, will be treated as a guest of the castle until the Queen arrives home."

Despite his fury, Lord Josiah could see that this would work to his advantage. Once he was on the inside of the castle, he just needed to await his opportunity and he would murder these upstarts in their beds. They were all that stood in his way to power. Once the Regent was dead and the Queen still absent, the army and people would soon fall into line. He was after all, a member of the royal family, albeit distant.

CHAPTER 24

"I demand to see my friends! That's the least you can allow me," Myriam shouted at Ghaffar.

"Of course, I assure you that they have not been harmed in any way. I also have good news for you." He was quite pleased with himself at how well this was all going. Four of the D'Anjue bloodline to feed his Empress would keep her alive for years to come. "Your grandmother is recovering, slightly, so we will arrange for her to share your room. How kind of our Empress to allow that, do you not agree?"

"If you think I will kneel to the likes of you, traitor, then think again," Myriam spat at him. She would personally take off this creature's head, if only she had a weapon. "I want answers about Ganry. Why have you taken him prisoner?"

"Come now, Queen Myriam, you know full well why. His and Perseus's actions in the royal chamber highlight the need to keep them restrained," Ghaffar replied, quite content with his reasoning. "We cannot be having any disturbances once we get started."

"Start what? What is it that you are about to start?" Myriam quizzed. "Why exactly have you tricked us to come to this wretched place?"

"This is my home and it is where you and your family will live out your days, so I'd advise you to get used to it. If you behave, we will keep you comfortable and allow you some freedom. All we ask in return is that you supply my Empress with your royal blood. Not too difficult a task, now that there are four of you."

As he finished speaking the door opened. Linz and Hendon walked in, with guards behind them pushing them on. Myriam ran to them both and hugged each one.

"I'm so glad you're both safe," she cried, tears now involuntarily running down her cheeks.

Linz wiped a tear away and looked into her eyes. It was not sadness that he saw in Myriam's face, but determination.

"I'm so sorry, Linz, that I brought you to this gruesome place," she sobbed onto his shoulder.

"I will leave you to console one another," Ghaffar spoke. "You should be grateful that my Empress is so generous to allow you all to converse." With that, he quickly turned and marched out of the room.

Myriam stopped her false tears. "I swear I will personally kill that creature," she promised. "We were right, they are wanting to feed from our bloodline. It must be what keeps the Empress alive. They intend to keep us for her for as long as possible, by taking a small amount from each of us in turn, so we stay healthy.

They must have bled my poor grandmother dry," she said, her anger boiling.

"I could find a weapon and ambush them as they come into the room, Myriam," Linz offered. "You never know, the confusion might open up an opportunity for us to escape and take our chances in the city."

"Linz, you are such a brave one, but no. I do believe that Perseus may our way out of this place. I don't know why, but I feel he came here for another reason and not just to bring me to my grandmother."

"It's a pity they took our daggers and rings," Linz said. "If we put the Berghein stones together we might have been strong enough to make an escape attempt."

"No," Hendon joined in the conversation. "Barnaby informs me that they are the keepers of these stones. They gave them to our ancestors in their hatred of the dragons. Then they cowardly sat back while our ancestors battled with the dragons. The Akkedis Empress allowed our family to keep these stones so she could spy on us through them. She has been kept alive by the lake men. Ghaffar, along with the Rooggaru, have been siphoning blood from our people to bring back to her."

Hendon cocked his head sideways, holding the staff close to his ear as though it were actually speaking to him physically. He nodded and muttered something unintelligible before continuing. "Barnaby also says that once all the stones were found and put together, this increased the power of the D'Anjue family and eroded the magic of the Akkedis Empress. She is weakened to a point of no return, and so she is dying. The only way to keep her alive now is with the untainted D'Anjue blood. The lake men's blood has become too weak for her needs. We are still linked to the royal family blood-line, so our blood is stronger and will keep her alive longer. For now, she does not need much but it will get worse. She will require more and more as time goes by. Once we die so will she."

"How does Barnaby know all this?" Myriam questioned.

"He tells me he has access to vast knowledge, more than he ever had. He looks things up, like we do in our library, or maybe even like a crystal ball, I'm not sure," Hendon tried to explain this strange information as best he could, but he did not fully understand it himself. Most of the time Barnaby spoke in riddles, using words he was unfamiliar with.

This was a revelation to them all and gave them renewed hope. With information like this it might just be the head start they needed over the Akkedis. They now knew their dark secrets.

"Excellent Hendon, you should thank Barnaby for me the next time you speak together. But, a word of caution. I would refrain from speaking to Ganry of this, you know what he is like on matters of magic and such. He would simply think you have lost your mind!"

CHAPTER 25

Ganry's body ached with a vengeance. This was not the first time he had been fastened in chains and hung on a wall but it had not happened to him in many years. Every muscle and every joint cried out for release.

Perseus was faring much better. Not only was he younger, but as soon as the guards left the room he shifted his body shape to that of the snake, allowing him to escape from his chains. Once he changed back into his human form he released Ganry for a short period.

"We cannot stay free for too long," Perseus warned. "They will be suspicious if we do not cry out in pain."

Once free of the chains, Ganry collapsed onto the floor in a heap. Free of his restraints he was sure the place stank even worse than it did when he was chained. An overpowering odor of urine, feces and dampness assaulted his senses, and to compound matters further, the air was so thick it was hardly breathable.

"I'm leaving this room for a short while to find water," Perseus told him. "I will be quick." And with that he was gone.

Ganry had no idea how he had managed to get out of the room as he had not been looking. He was busy regulating his breathing, taking in as much air in as possible. This truly was a dungeon, deep in the bowels of the earth.

As he sat up, leaning his aching back against the hard stone wall, he noticed a huge hole in the floor. Now he knew how Perseus had slithered out of the room. The shape-shifter could dig tunnels, just like the sand worms. He hoped Perseus had an idea how to fill this tunnel in when he returned. As he sat there pondering the problem, the snake's head appeared in the hole.

The huge snake slithered back into the room and used its tail to replace a mound of earth back into the tunnel. Then, altered into that of a human male, handed Ganry a pouch of water.

Ganry guzzled half, though he knew he should not drink so fast. But caution was the last thing on his mind. Handing the rest of the water back to Perseus, he was feeling much better already.

Perseus drank slower, not needing as much refreshment as the human.

"Are you going to tell me your tale then, Perseus?" he asked of his companion.

"My master is Qutaybah, I have not any more to tell," he replied, clearly not over willing to reveal his history.

Ganry tried a different line of questioning. "What kind of creature are you?"

"I am a Suggizon. My master saved me from being devoured, so I owe him my life."

"And? The story is?" Ganry was determined he would have some explanation.

Perseus sighed, closing his eyes briefly. "My people live in the mountains of Vandemland," he began. "We are a rarity and considered quite a delicacy in our reptile form. I was captured when I was quite young and traded on the slave market. I refused to Change from human, so the slavers beat me. When we are angry, we cannot stop the Change. Once changed I caused havoc in the market place, killing a number of slave traders. After I was recaptured I was to be beheaded, but Master Qutaybah offered them a price they could not refuse. I have been with him since, and I serve him loyally."

"These are strange lands indeed," Ganry commented, his voice hoarse from the thick, stinking air.

"I hear footsteps approaching. I must tie you back up again," Perseus said, standing up quickly.

As soon as Ganry was back in position, Perseus changed form and wriggled into his own chains. Seconds later they heard keys rattling in the lock and in walked Ghaffar.

"I bear good news for you, Ganry," Ghaffar said. The former mercenary lifted up his chin that had been dangling to touch his chest. "My wonderful and benevolent Empress is allowing the Duchess to share a room with your Queen."

"Forgive me if I cannot smile," he replied, gruffly. "Your Empress amazes me with her kindness."

"Indeed!" Ghaffar agreed, knowing full well what Ganry's caustic comments meant. "I am here to ask of you some small questions," Ghaffar continued. "I am sure you will be glad to keep your Queen safe, and so will be willing to answer honestly."

There was an empty silence hanging in the air as no one spoke. Ganry would not waste his small amount of energy on this fiend.

"When you set off on your quest, exactly who was aware that you were visiting with the Akkedis?" Ghaffar asked.

Ganry did not reply. Instead he laughed quietly until his laugh echoed loudly around the stone wall chamber.

"You fear an attack, my little friend?" Ganry asked, when he had finished laughing. "Oh, I assure you, you will get one," Ganry promised.

Ghaffar smiled and then stood aside, allowing a tall female Akkedis into the cell. She was dressed in a light tunic which had many woven pouches. Within the pouches, Ganry could see moving dark shapes.

"This is Sileta, she is the keeper of the kewers," Ghaffar said, with a smirk of satisfaction in his features. "Our kewers are a special creature which only Sileta can control. Have you heard of a kewer, human?"

Ganry did not reply, instead he simply stared fiercely into the eyes of the little man.

"I will take your silence as ignorance and I will explain this insect in its simplicity," Ghaffar answered to the silent Ganry. "It is such a tiny thing, with a long piercing snout, and, like the Akkedis, feeds from blood. But this creature digs into its host and makes its way to the heart, and once there it will feed until the heart ceases to pump. Then it will leave the host and find another. You see, the kewers like their blood warm and straight from the source. Now, Sileta here, she can talk to her pets and she can call them to come back to her, and they do as she asks, even if they are just about to feed on the pumping heart. She is a good mother to them and cares that they are fed with only the best, and they are loyal to her."

Sileta then gave Ganry an exhibition of her pets. She called to them by singing a light melody, and in moments her entire body was covered with a sheen of shimmering blue and green luster. It appeared that her skin was moving as they slithered along, running around their keeper's body.

"I would like Sileta to introduce her pets to your heart, Ganry, where they would feed until it stops, unless you feel you can answer my questions before this happens?" Ghaffar announced. "But first, perhaps a little demonstration will help loosen your tongue."

He turned to the female Akkedis. "Sileta, if you will?"

Sileta hummed her tune louder and danced lightly. As she increased the tempo of her dancing and humming, the kewers began to make clicking sounds which grew louder and louder. She danced closer to Ganry and draped an arm over his shoulder, releasing some of the kewers onto his naked skin.

As soon as they landed on him, he felt a sharp pinch as they buried themselves under his skin. The pain was excruciating as he could feel the pathway that they took on their journey in his body, and the stinging sensation felt like his body was burning from within.

Sileta moved her arms away and finished her dance, making strange noises. Ganry could hardly open his eyes to watch her. She had left her pets running riot inside his body. He shivered with a cold sweat, his entire body felt like a raw nerve that was being tugged upon and twisted. Finally, he succumbed to the pain and cried out in agony.

Sileta changed her tune slightly and the small bugs appeared upon Ganry's skin. They fell to the floor and scampered back to their keeper, disappointed that they had not been allowed to feast. Sileta left the room.

"I leave you to rest, human. I'm sure that Sileta's little pets will have worn you out." Ghaffar smiled as he spoke. "I will bring her with me to visit you again, only next time, if you do not have the answers that I require then your Queen may no longer have her gallant bodyguard."

Ghaffar quickly turned and left the room.

Ganry and Perseus were alone, once again.

CHAPTER 26

Myriam awoke feeling quite refreshed. The female Akkedis servant, Arriba, was in her room, putting out a fresh jug of water and a bowl for her to wash before breakfast.

"How do you know when it's night or day down here in your city, Arriba?" Myriam asked, trying to strike up a conversation. She had tried many times to befriend Arriba, but none had been successful.

"We can tell by the air vents," she replied.

Myriam was surprised to have an answer, so she pushed her luck even further.

"Is my door locked? I would like to visit with my friends," she asked the Akkedis servant.

"Friends? They are your family, are they not?" Arriba responded.

Myriam laughed at the thought of Linz and Hendon being her brothers.

"We are of the same bloodline, yes, but I suspect we are far removed from being direct relations," Myriam answered, and the Akkedis was puzzled.

"I have heard of humans having families. My people do not have such things. I would have no idea who has my blood," Arriba said quietly, as if she did not want to be heard saying such a thing.

Arriba was being quite talkative today and Myriam encouraged her to continue.

"Once we are born and we hatch from our eggs, we stay in the nursery until we can join society and become a productive worker. We do not know who parented us. We know of loyalty to our leaders, but not of this love that humans have."

"Then you have done well to understand the concept of a human family, Arriba," Myriam remarked.

"We are all schooled to understand the world around us," Arriba explained.

"Do the Akkedis not fall in love, as in a male and a female?" Myriam asked, thinking they still had to mate to produce the eggs.

"I cannot answer that." Arriba's attitude changed at that question. She seemed upset and slammed the door as she left the room.

Myriam was left wondering what she had said to upset her.

Quickly she washed and dressed. The Akkedis had provided some basic tunics for day and night knowing that humans liked to change, which was something they did not practice much themselves. She appreciated that in some respects, the Akkedis were trying to make them comfortable. They supplied them good food and clean clothing, easing their imprisonment somewhat. This reminded her of Ganry, and she wondered how he fared. She doubted they would kill him or Perseus, and today she intended on demanding a visit with them.

Knocking on the door of Linz and Hendon, there was no reply. Whilst she was allowed freedom within the shared corridor that led to all of their rooms, the guards still manned it and watched her closely. She wondered at what the guards must think she was about. It was not as if she could run and escape this hell hole. No matter, she simply turned the handle and entered the room.

It was dark inside with no means of lighting whatsoever. She went to the pots that held the crystals which shone with light and removed the covers. The brightness soon reflected around the room, and now she could see that her friends were still asleep.

"I thought we were going to make some demands today," she said in an extra loud voice, yet still they did not stir. "You're both going to have to wake up!" she yelled even louder this time.

For all her efforts, both the young men simply groaned and turned over in their beds. Linz pulled his cover over his head, because of the light.

"Whatever is the matter?" she asked as she yanked the cover from his head.

"They started to take our blood and it makes us tired," he replied, hoping this would mean that Myriam would leave them alone.

"We have to fight this, to stay strong. I think we will need some training, of sorts, to keep our strength up," she suggested.

"Easy for you to say." Hendon's voice came from under his blankets. "They haven't started to eat you yet. I think you must be dessert," he finished, a light muffled laugh coming from beneath his covers.

"I'm going to tell Ghaffar that if they want us to stay strong, to provide blood for his glorious Empress, then we need Ganry to keep us fighting fit," she told them both.

"I do hope to keep you healthy, but not fighting," a different voice came from the doorway that Myriam had left slightly ajar.

She knew who's voice it was without even turning around. Ghaffar was becoming a permanent feature in their daily lives. There he stood, his billowing cape and his ugly face. Determined to have her way, she approached him at speed, until she was talking almost into his face.

"We must have Ganry returned to us, Ghaffar," she said, facing the little man as close as she wanted to put herself. He stank of some unsavory aroma. "He is the only one who can keep us healthy."

"I have better news than that for you, human Queen." Ghaffar looked pleased with himself. "If you care to go your own room, you have a visitor."

Myriam guessed who it was and rushed across the corridor back to her room. There, sat in a large armchair still looking quite frail, was her grandmother.

"Grandmother, I am so pleased to see you looking well," she said, as she knelt at the Duchess' feet and hugged her legs.

"Oh, my dear, do be careful," the Duchess said quietly, wondering if her frail body could withstand a young woman hugging her so tightly. "You have a strong grip, so at least they have not harmed you yet," she said, relieved.

"No," Myriam said sadly as she pulled away. "They started on my dear friends first. Hendon says I am to be dessert."

The Duchess was amused by this and laughed for the first time in such a long while.

"Dear, dear girl, it gladdens my heart to be with you. They say I can stay, so I should be up and about in no time," the Duchess assured her.

Myriam smiled, watching the Duchess as she crooked her finger, beckoning Myriam to come closer.

"You must tell me everything. Together we will create a plan for your escape," she whispered in her granddaughter's ear.

"Grandmother, there is plenty of time for that. I intend on keeping us all healthy. This must please the Akkedis Empress as it means we'll live longer. There will be time soon enough to plan our escape." She whispered the last part. "Once I have Ganry returned to me."

CHAPTER 27

Lord Josiah was quite enjoying his imprisonment. Though he could not leave the castle, he did have the freedom of its walls. He was provided with many luxuries consisting of an apartment of rooms, and quality food and drink. All along with a manservant. It would do, for now, while he plotted and planned his next move.

Sitting on a veranda that overlooked a lake, he feasted on a fine breakfast. With his army gone, he laughed to himself, thinking that he did not need them to rid him of this supposed Regent. All he needed to do was await his closest advisors to visit him, and then he could implement a plot to rid the kingdom of this upstart.

A knock at his door pulled him from his conspiratorial thoughts, but he did not get up to answer it. Why should he, that was his a servants job. He remained out on the veranda, enjoying the sun and the food, when he became overshadowed by the arrival of a group of people.

Turning around to see who has come to bother him, hc relaxes at the sight of his advisers. Now the time had come. At last he could speak his thoughts with others, and see what ideas they have come up with in plotting the demise of the young man who calls himself a Regent.

"Come, come," he says, "let us not waste time. We must have a plan and quickly. I want to be sat upon that throne within days. Have you thought of any solutions yet, Lexx, I'm relying on your expertise to deal with this situation quickly," he asked of his closest advisor.

"The people are nervous, Lord, you should tread carefully," Lexx warned him, cautiously. "They do not forget the last usurper and the damage he did to the Kingdom."

"Pah!" Lord Josiah exclaimed. "The only usurper around here is that upstart, Artas. The Queen had no right to place an outsider in such a position. I will run this Kingdom until her return. If I can prevent her return, then all the better. We need to be discovering exactly what madness had over taken her to cause her to leave the throne so unprotected. This Kingdom needs a powerful leader, such as myself, not a frivolous slip of a girl."

"If you are seen to be grasping the throne by force, it will be considered as an act of war against the Queen's wishes, and she has many allies," his advisor said, wisely. "You would do better to befriend this boy first, find out where the Queen has gone. As you say, maybe once we know where she is then we can ensure she never returns."

"Hmm, as always you make a point," Josiah conceded with a laugh. "Your mind is even more twisted than my own. That's why I like you, Lexx. We are of the same mind you and I, but you always have a clearer head."

Lexx bowed to his Lord, knowing that one day he would out maneuver him and take over his entire estate, or even his Kingdom, if they can pull this off.

"I suggest you apologize, sire," Lexx advised, knowing that Josiah was an expert at groveling. "Make the boy think you regret your actions and then stay on in the castle and befriend him. Try and join his circle of elite advisors. Once we know where Myriam is, we can put your plans into action. The boy could have a tragic accident, and you would rule in his place. Awaiting a Queen who would never return. Within six months the Kingdom could be yours."

"Yes, yes, I will make my apologies this very day, and take our first steps to the throne of Palara."

"Well, I don't trust him," Leonie said, as they discussed Lord Josiah's official apology. "Why would he wish to stay on in the castle?"

"Ever the interrogator," Artas laughed at her.

He had been somewhat surprised that Josiah had pulled out of his attempt to take over the throne, but it was sensible. His advisors had probably forced his hand.

"We cannot simply turn him out, he is a relative of the Queen, after all," Parsival stated. "I'm afraid we're stuck with him for as long as he wishes to stay."

"Well, do not seat him with me for dinner," Leonie remarked. "I refuse to have anything to do with the little weasel. What I will be doing, though, is keeping a very close eye on him. I simply do not trust him or that advisor of his."

"You mean Lexx Farrow?" Artas knew the man to be nothing but an accountant. "I don't suppose you go from counting money to advising the one who provides the money by being dishonest. Surely he can be trusted?"

"No one who has anything to do with Lord Josiah, is ever to be trusted in my eyes," Leonie said. "Fear not, Artas, I will have my spies watching their every move."

CHAPTER 28

"That is all she asked me to tell you," Arriba informed Ganry, readying herself to throw the bucket of cold water over his body.

"I appreciate your daily cleansing methods, Arriba," Ganry told her, smiling, "but this is more important. If you are able to let me know how my companions are, I would appreciate that even more."

"I have just told you," she said, becoming impatient with the human. "I do not understand what more you require of me?"

"Are you taking her blood yet?" he dared to ask. He hoped this would not put her off speaking with him. It had already come as a surprise when she informed him that she had news from the Queen.

"Only the two men provide blood for my Empress at the moment. Ghaffar's plan is to leave Queen Myriam until the last, hoping that under her care the Duchess will thrive again and once more provide another source of blood."

Arriba was fast becoming nervous, glancing around the cell and listening at the door to hear if the two guards were near, but they paid her no attention. If Ghaffar was to learn that she was sending secret communications between the human Queen and her soldier, he would have her killed, of this she was certain.

"And the men, Linz and Hendon, are they well?" he asked.

"They sleep a lot. My Empress cannot keep her strength up with their blood alone though. I fear that she will demand the purer supply soon. If the Duchess is not well enough, then it will come from your Queen. I should say no more. Please, if I am found to be speaking with you, I will be put to my death for treason."

Ganry nodded his head and smiled at Arriba, and thanked her for the information. This was a worrying turn of events. They would need to find a way out of here soon, before Myriam was too weak to leave.

His body suddenly shook in shock as the cold water rained down on him. Arriba had done her duty of drenching his battered body and cleansing his wounds. It may have been his imagination, but he felt that the water was a little warmer today.

Arriba repeated her task with Perseus and then left the cell.

Perseus shook his head to rid himself of the excess water in his long hair. He also appreciated the water and the information.

"Can you not do something to go and check on them?" Ganry knew he asked much, but the daily torture of the kewers was causing him to weaken. If he was not out of this cell soon, then he would be no use to Myriam at all.

"Could you not tell them what you know, Ganry, or simply tell them a lie?" Perseus asked. "Ease your suffering, my friend. I fear you cannot withstand this torture much longer."

He would die before he would give any information to the Akkedis that might give them an advantage. Perseus was helping all he could, for now, by finding him extra food and water, and releasing him from his shackles every time he had endured the torment of the insects.

It was obvious what Ghaffar was wanting. He needed confirmation that the humans in the Kingdom were not aware that their Queen had visited the Akkedis city. This could bring war between the two cities and that would ruin any chances of their survival.

Ganry was not allowing the Akkedis the luxury of such peace of mind. In fact, many knew that they had come here, though not all, but certainly Qutaybah was aware. Ganry could only hope that sooner or later, Qutaybah may come in search of his slave, Perseus. Perseus, on his part, would give him no information on whether his master might follow him or not.

"Yes, the thought of lying had crossed my mind, but I hate to give that creature any satisfaction whatsoever. And besides, I fear our death may follow such a confession."

Perseus nodded his agreement. He knew that Ganry was correct. It was the search of information that kept them both alive. Once they had no use for them, they would be surplus to requirements and quickly dispatched. As much as it pained Perseus to see Ganry suffer so, it was to his advantage. The longer he could hold out, the more he could discover about the caves in this city.

Perseus could not tell Ganry all that he knew, as he was sworn by his master not to reveal his real mission with anyone. Qutaybah, his master, was an outlaw with an army of mercenaries, but he was a good man in his heart. He had saved Perseus from death and had always treated him with respect in the years he had been with him. This was his opportunity to pay back that kindness.

Whilst his mission was to aid Queen Myriam in her quest, he had also a secret task for his master. Qutaybah was aware of the vast riches the Akkedis had in their mines, riches they jealously guarded and shared with no one. It was his master's intention to take those mines for himself, and Perseus was here to facilitate that.

"I am ready to take you to visit your Queen," he told Ganry. "Then maybe you will stop all your complaining."

"Complaining? I am a warrior, I do not complain, I merely tell you of my opinions."

"I must warn you, Ganry, we can only be free a short while and must return to these shackles. It is not yet time for our escape. I take you only because you are in need of encouragement. I see you flagging every time those cursed insects enter your body. You just need to hold on a little more. Soon we will be free and you can extract your revenge on the Akkedis."

CHAPTER 29

Ganry awoke with a start as he felt his shackles being removed.

"It is only me, Ganry. It is time, if you still wish to visit your Queen," Perseus said while loosening his chains. Once free he slumped to the floor, his legs temporarily unable to support him.

"How do you do that?" Ganry asked. "Are you some magic being? You shake off your shackles easily and you can shape shift into a giant snake. I'm glad you're my ally and not my foe."

Perseus smiled at him. "You haven't seen me eat a body yet," he said, a wicked twinkle in his eye.

Ganry knew he was not joking. He'd seen the giant snake and it was more than capable of swallowing a body whole.

"Come, we do not have much time." Perseus rushed Ganry once he was able to stand. "I do not wish to alarm the Akkedis too soon. I will transform back into the snake and you must hold onto my tail as I make my way through the tunnel. I have already burrowed while you rested. It is very dark and there's little room in there. You will feel enclosed within a tiny confinement but it will only bc for a few moments. Are you ready?"

Ganry nodded and watched in awe as Persues Changed from a tall muscular man into a huge snake, right before his eyes. The transformation was instantaneous. The snake's body was wider than the thickness of a human, and its length was at least ten feet.

It slithered about the floor before gathering up in a coil, its scales shimmering in the candlelight. It raised up to Ganry's height, putting its face level with his, and hissed at him. A forked tongue slipped in and out of its mouth before it quickly turned and dived into the tunnels. It moved so fast that Ganry almost missed the tail, but he lunged just at the last moment and was dragged into the darkness of the earthy hole.

It seemed an age to Ganry that they were twisting and turning through the ground with him clinging on desperately to the snakes tail. The tunnel was only just wide enough to accommodate his body, and the walls bumped and rubbed against his skin as they quickly passed through the tunnel. Eventually, he could see light up ahead as they both exited the end. He realized that they had arrived into Perseus's room, the one he had occupied before they were imprisoned. It was the same one where he had met the snake under the bed.

Ganry clambered out of the hole and under the bed, then stood up and brushed off the dirt from his body. The snake turned back into its human form.

"It has taken me much adventuring to find the best way. I have spent many a night wandering through tunnels looking for options of the safest route for both of us," Perseus whispered.

"I wish you would share with me exactly what your intentions are, Perseus. Perhaps I can aid you." He tried his luck, though he knew it was pointless.

"In time, all will be revealed, but the less you know the better. Then you cannot tell our mutual enemy anything as he tortures your body."

Ganry had to admit that was probably a good idea. Ghaffar never relented in finding any excuse to put those creatures underneath his skin. The fact that he was still alive was making him believe that Ghaffar was actually enjoying watching his personal agony far too much.

"I will have my revenge on that monster," he assured Perseus.

"We will all have our revenge when the time is right. For now, we have other things on our minds. The Duchess sleeps in your room and Linz and Hendon are still sharing. We will enter the Queen's room. Are you ready, Ganry?"

"Indeed, I am," he said, breathing a sigh of relief that at last he could talk to Myriam and know she was fighting fit.

They stood at the other side of Myriam's door in Perseus's old room, listening. The Duchess slept soundly in her bed in Ganry's old room. Once they were certain that Myriam was alone, Ganry slowly opened the door and glanced in.

He could see Myriam sitting up in her bed with her bedside light still shining. Looking closer, he could see that she had fallen asleep in that position, her body sup-

ported by a pile of pillows. He looked upon her inno-
cent face. It seemed strained and pale. She probably
slept like this every night, on guard and nervous.

He quietly entered her room and quickly crosscd to
the bed, but she did not stir. He gently shook her shoulder and she moaned in her sleep. He had expected her
to awaken with a start. It seemed a shame to wake her
up when she slept so deeply.

"My Queen," he whispered as he leaned down to her
ear. "It is me, Ganry. Wake up, I need to speak with
you."

She mumbled his name, but she was still in a slumber. As her arm fell forward he noticed the puncture
marks on her skin. The bastards had started on her already. This sleep was not a natural one but induced
upon her as they drained her blood. His anger quickly
rose. Had Ghaffar been present now, he would gladly
have killed him with his bare hands, regardless of the
consequences. Finally she opened her eyes and upon
seeing Ganry, she smiled.

"Ganry, is it really you or am I dreaming?" she
asked, sleepily.

"Perseus has managed to find a way to get me here,"
he kept his voice low, not wanting any of the guards to
hear anything.

He stroked her pale skin, once again remembering
his own daughter, Ruby. His love for his Queen was
purely paternal, and he hated that the lizards of this city
were hurting her.

She shot up, suddenly realizing it was all real.

"Oh, Ganry, Ganry, it really is you?" she said in a
loud whisper.

"Yes, I am here, you are not alone in this," he assured her. "Hang on in there. Soon, I promise, all this will be over," he tried to reassure her, but inside himself he was unsure how it would all end. He had confidence in Perseus, but would they all live through this, he was not too sure.

"How are Linz and Hendon baring up?" he asked her.

"They are constantly tired and now the Akkedis Empress is demanding my blood every other day. Arriba tells me she takes two measures of their blood one day, and then one measure of mine, the next. I tire very quickly on the days that they drain me. They were here earlier today."

"And the Duchess?" Ganry asked.

"The Duchess is probably healthier than any of her rescuers," a female voice said behind him.

He rose up from his knees beside Myriam, and looked upon the old lady. She was quite right, she looked in far better health than when he had last looked upon her in her own room.

"I'm glad that they're leaving you alone for now," he said, but with a little regret for in his heart he wished they would not feed upon Myriam. "You must keep yourselves as healthy as you can and stay ready, for soon we shall have our revenge upon these reptiles."

"You have a plan?" Myriam asked, still whispering, for fear of alerting the guards.

"My friend here is the one with the plan," Ganry turned to Perseus, who was bowing down to the Duchess.

What happened next shocked Ganry. The Duchess approached Perseus and embraced him.

"Perseus, my dear, dear friend. I knew Qutaybah would not let me down," she said to him, a tear in her eye.

CHAPTER 30

Lord Josiah was unaware that he was being watched. He never thought for one moment that the boy Artas would have a spy network up and running. He assumed he was quite safe going about with his plotting and scheming, with little or no caution.

Already he had managed to find some information, in that the girl had gone searching for her grandmother. She had taken her closest bodyguard, who was a seasoned and respected mercenary, so she must have had a destination. It is doubtful that she went wandering around endlessly in her search. He now needed to find out where this journey had taken her.

Rumors in his own network of spies indicated that she had been seen in disguise at the borders, awaiting to cross into Vandemland. Most had been fooled, but there had been one sly merchant who knew exactly who she was, and he had sold his information at a high cost to the Lord's spy.

Queen Myriam was somewhere in Vandemland. It would only be a matter of time before he knew of her ultimate destination.

Meanwhile, he would play the fool, let this boy think he was regretful over his actions and stayed on only to make amends. The boy had foolishly allowed him more freedom, saying he was welcome to stay at the castle as long as he liked. Either the boy was totally incompetent or too merciful for his own good. Whatever the reasons for his kindness, Lord Josiah would take the fullest advantage of it.

Sat on his balcony that overlooked a lake, he was about to enjoy the luxuries of an expensive tobacco in his pipe when Lexx burst through the door to his apartment.

"We have her sire, we know exactly where she has gone," he cried out, shutting the door behind him so none would hear their secrets.

"Well, go on then man, what is so urgent that you burst into my chambers and give your Lord such a stir?" Lord Josiah asked, keen to hear the news.

"She has gone to the Akkedis city, Lord Josiah," his man informed him, as if this was the answer to everything.

"Good god man, why is that good? I have no idea where those stinking creatures live," Josiah replied, disappointed at the information.

"I have not told you all yet, sire," Lexx burst forth in excitement, once again. "Word is out that Ghaffar of the Lizards, is seeking connections with those in Palara who hold some influence and would benefit from the Queen never returning. I paid a high price for this information, Lord, and it could be to your best advantage to be the first to respond. There is no more Lord as deserving as you, sire," he finished.

"I've met that slimy creature before and he is not to be trusted," Josiah responded. "How are we to contact him? I will not go to that stinking place of Vandemland."

"I am way ahead of you, sire," Lexx bragged.

"Yes, yes, man, get on with it then." Josiah was becoming impatient with the amount of time it was taking to get all the information out of his man today.

"I have set communications in motion to pass word to this Ghaffar that we are interested in his proposition. Now we know where the Queen is, that gives us an advantage, but we must be quick to act. There are others in Palara who would be happy to deal with Ghaffar."

Lexx made himself comfortable on a chair opposite Lord Josiah, looking smug at his achievements.

"Well, get on with it then, man!" Lord Josiah shouted at him. "You don't have time to dally smoking my tobacco. Go and ensure our success, we do not want any others jumping in front of us. Who knows what part of my family will be seeking to take the throne from this child. I want a deal sealed with this lizard man as soon as possible. Off you go."

Lexx jumped up and saluted his Lord, although a little disappointed that he was not celebrating in praise. Of course, Lord Josiah was quite correct, a deal needed to be secured and once his Lord was King, he would yield many benefits for all his efforts.

"I may need some gold, sire, if I am to do business with the Narcs," he said.

"I pay you well. Use your own gold and if all turns out, I will compensate you tenfold," his Lord commanded.

Lexx was not too keen on paying with his own purse. If it all fell through he would be heavily out of pocket. Still, if it all worked as he planned, soon he would be the right hand man of a King.

CHAPTER 31

Qutaybah was relaxing on cushions and drinking his favorite tea. It had been a long hard day, attending many meetings with his network of smugglers and traders, and there should be only one more matter to see to.

He had agreed to see a mercenary who had come out of the desert requesting a meeting. His personal interest in the desert people meant that he would not refuse. Many of them worked for him, transporting his goods all over Vandemland. One of his best men, Perseus, was on a very important mission there. He hoped the news was not about Perseus as he had no news of him for a few days, and this was concerning.

The flaps of his tent were pushed to one side and a tall tan skinned man entered his temporary abode.

"Dramand, my friend, I had not realized it was you." Qutaybah smiled, always pleased to see old acquaintances who have done much work for him in the past.

"What brings you to my part of the world? Surely we have far too much rain for you here," he laughed.

"Well, at this time of the seasons, I know I will stay dry, Qutaybah." He grinned back and sat down on the cushions opposite.

Qutaybah personally poured him some orange tea, happy to spend time with a good man.

"I do not know if you presently have ongoing business with the Akkedis, Qutaybah?" he began, and noted Qutaybah's features take on a seriousness. "I hear that one of the leaders, known as Ghaffar, is seeking intelligence in the human underworld with regards to Queen Myriam. I know of your fondness for the Duchess D'Anjue, who is related to the the royal family, so wondered if it was wise to seek your advice?"

"It is always wise to seek my advice in all matters, Dramand, but, yes, I do have a personal interest in this and a particular fondness in this family. Tell me more." Qutaybah wondered why he had not yet had this information already. His spy network was second to none.

"The message is aimed at influential humans who may wish to see the Queen come to harm. With my curiosity piqued, I sent in one of my men to dig a little deeper." He paused for breath and Qutaybah leaned closer to him, not wanting to miss anything.

"For some reason they wish to spread a message that Queen Myriam has died in an accident in Vandemland. My sources tell me that the Queen is actually away from the castle, but this information has only just been publicly announced. I have to wonder why the Akkedis would be interested in the humans, let alone the Queen?"

"It is indeed a conundrum," Qutaybah replied. "I'm glad you have a man in this as we can use him to filter out this Ghaffar. He is one who I would wish to be rid of, once and for all. Tell me, has anyone responded to this request from the Kingdom, do you know?"

"Yes, I just received word today that a Lord Josiah is willing to do business with Ghaffar." Dramand stopped, and smiled. "Strangely, rumors are abound regarding a group of humans and a scuffle in the Akkedis Empress' chambers. Now, under normal circumstances I would have thought that unlikely as outsiders never gain access to the Akkedis city, let alone a human." He shook his head as if agreeing that this was indeed an impossibility. "But now I see you are involved, perhaps it is not so unlikely after all?"

"Ahhh." Qutaybah put up his hands, palms outwards as if to admit it was all his fault. "That would be my doing."

"Surely, even the great Qutaybah cannot possibly infiltrate the Akkedis Empress' city, let alone her chambers?" Dramand knew that Qutaybah's reach was long, but this far?

"I have my methods, Dramand. You, more than any other, should know that. We go back a long way. Will you help me to squash these irritants?" Qutaybah asked. "This Lord Josiah needs teaching a lesson or two as well, especially if he threatens the human royal family who I consider my allies. And, as for the elusive Ghaffar, he needs to be eliminated once and for all. Long has he caused mischief in Vandemland, and yet he always manages to slip through my fingers. It is high time those gems were spread about Vandemland more equally, do you not agree?"

"I have no love for the Akkedis," Dramand admitted. "However, I have an immense fondness of everything that sparkles, especially of the valuable type."

Both men laughed at this. "You and me both, Dramand," Qutaybah said. "We can agree upon this."

Qutaybah could not be happier. He had planned to march onto the Akkedis city the very next day, with a good portion of his army of mercenaries. With Dramand's men too, they would be a formidable force and it would greatly increase his chances of success.

"So, great leader of great mercenaries, what is it you are plotting that I have missed, so far?" Dramand asked, realizing that Qutaybah was already knee deep in this tale.

"Well, how about the opening of the Akkedis mines? I understand they are full of precious gems, but the Akkedis keep it all to themselves. Many emissaries I have sent to negotiate a trade agreement, and many an emissary has never returned. If we could take those mines, we would be richer than our wildest dreams."

Dramand clapped his hands together as he could not contain his excitement at such news.

"You would go on such an adventure without me?" he asked.

"My friend, it is not just for wealth I take this action. I have a personal involvement in the human royal family and would like to see them returned safely," Qutaybah admitted, honestly. "I have also sent one of my best men in there, in the hope that he may get an opportunity to strike at the Akkedis Empress."

"Your personal involvements are mine too," Dramand informed him. "Together we will see your allies released, and our purses bulging. When do we start?"

"I go tomorrow. The Akkedis have ruled that part of the desert long enough. It is time we showed them that, in this land, we share."

Both men raised their glasses in salute, and drank to their partnership and their upcoming venture.

CHAPTER 32

Myriam was forever tired, although they were now taking blood from the Duchess too, which provided her with some respite. She wasn't happy that they were starting on the Duchess again, but her grandmother insisted. "We need you at full strength," is all she would say on the matter.

Linz and Hendon were still being used, but they had large amounts taken and not very often. Between the four of them, they were managing to feed the Akkedis Empress, for now.

"This cannot go on forever, grandmother," she complained to the Duchess.

"Oh, it will not need to dear, you just need to be patient. Our rescuers will arrive soon." The Duchess was adamant that all would be well, in the end.

"Well, I hope it is before one of us dies. I have no idea how Ganry and Perseus are doing. They haven't visited for a while and that makes me worry all the more. I have no idea why Ghaffar keeps them alive, and if I did, I may have some leverage in their keep. I have threatened to stop allowing my blood to be taken, but they simply say they'll force me anyway. The servant girl, Arriba, hasn't been around for a long time either. I cant help but feel that this is all very foreboding."

"You should try and do something to take your mind off of all of this. You could sew with me." The Duchess lifted the tapestry off her knee that she was mindlessly creating. "I find it relaxes my tensions."

"No, I don't think it would help grandmother, I was never any good at crafts," she admitted. "The last time I spoke with Ganry and Perseus, we agreed to discuss an escape plan, but they have not been back since. Perhaps they were caught escaping their cell. I do believe that Perseus could escape from this place single handedly. I don't know how he does it, but he seems to be very talented at the art of escape," Myriam finished, her thoughts now wandering off to Perseus.

"He is a Suggizon," the Duchess informed her.

"A what? What is that? I suppose it must be a tribe of warriors within Vandemland, is it?"

"Come and sit by my side, Myriam, and listen to me," the Duchess suggested. "I don't wish to shout to you across the chamber."

Myriam sat in a comfortable chair, thinking that it must have been brought in to the city for the humans only, as an Akkedis would not fit in it. Then she wondered the same about the beds and other furniture.

"Your mind is wandering, Myriam, and I need you to concentrate on what I tell you," the Duchess said, quietly.

Myriam looked at her grandmother, who had been such a formidable woman in her youth, and indeed not so long ago during the coupe of the royal family. Now, she was looking old and weak.

"Myriam!" she heard the Duchess's voice shout her name, and jumped with surprise. "Your mind wanders, child. It is the lack of blood in your brain, I'm sure of it. Now listen to me. Perseus is from a rare breed of snake men. He can shape shift into a giant snake. I know of this because he works for Qutaybah, as you know."

"Yes," Myriam said, listening to her grandmother's words. "I have a vague memory of the Suggizon from my history lessons, now I think of it. I thought them legends, not real?" she questioned.

"I have seen him change with my own eyes. He is very real, though there were not many of his kind left. Those that survived were secreted far away by Qutaybah so they could be left in peace to breed. Hopefully, he has saved the species. The few that are caught these days are eaten as a rare dish, would you believe, by barbarians." The Duchess was clearly angry at the very thought. "I knew that Qutaybah was trying to increase the population but that was years ago. I must admit I never queried over the progress of that project."

"I thought Qutaybah was a slaver and leader of mercenaries?"

"He is not a man to be double crossed, that's for sure," the Duchess replied. "If he sent you here, then there will be more to the plan. Otherwise he would have come himself. I doubt he would have known that the Empress wanted our family blood for her own personal supply. When I can talk to Perseus again, I will find out why he is here. If he was meant simply to be your guide, he would have left you at the stones you told me of, the ones where the sand worms attacked you. There was no reason for him to go any further. You had the Akkedis to show you the way."

"I do believe you are correct, grandmother," Myriam agreed, thinking her grandmother to be very clever. "You think that Qutaybah had another objective in mind?"

"Indeed, he has other investments in this project, I guarantee you that, which is good because it should align with our interests," Duchess D'Anjue said reassuringly. "We just need to survive long enough."

CHAPTER 33

The temporary camp was busily packing away. They had been told that a long journey lay ahead and the troops were readying themselves to cross the desert. Pans clanged, hammers banged on wooden poles, and voices chattered. Women folded the washed and dried clothes from the previous day and packed up the food rations. Everyone seemingly had a task to do, or they would not have been required to join the troops. Qutaybah kept his slaves busy. There was no time for leisure and no time to waste.

"I know this is the way, Dramand, because I was the one who led them here many years ago," he told his desert friend.

"Those are not easy mountains to be crossing. It could take us all year."

"We do not need to go all the way as we have arranged a small holding here," he said, pointing his finger to a place in the desert on the map. "We built a village so that the Suggizon would know of anyone attempting to cross the mountain pass that hides their people. This village consists of humans, mainly. There should be a Suggizon on duty, so they can send a message fast to the town hidden in the mountains. For all I know, it could be a city now. I have not visited in many years and Perseus tells me, very proudly, that it has grown."

"I think we had better stop talking and get moving. We have a long way to go. Though why you insist on these people being involved is beyond me," Dramand complained as he rolled up the large scrolled maps.

"I promised Perseus that if he killed the Akkedis Empress it would make his people rich. They will have a part of the gem mines."

"By the time you have given all the parts of the gem mines away, there will be none left for those of us doing all the work," Dramand complained again.

"Bah, there is plenty to go around. These people need to find a trade to enhance their population. Did you know they were almost extinct when I found Perseus?" Qutaybah exclaimed.

"Your heart is too soft," Dramand laughed, knowing it to be true. Qutaybah was a hard, but fair man. He was not seen as cruel, but those who crossed him would soon feel his wrath.

"If the plan is to drive the Akkedis out of their city, then we will need more men than we have here," Qutaybah informed Dramand. "I have already dispatched riders to Palara. They will warn the Regent of the betrayal and plotting between Ghaffar and Lord Josiah. I am also hoping as a result of this news, he will send some of his best troops to help in the rescue of his

Queen, and join us in battle at the Akkedis city. With our men combined, humans and the mighty Suggizon, I am certain victory will be ours. Do you agree, my friend, that are we going to make ourselves rich?"

Qutaybah did not wait for an answer. He climbed onto the seat of his camel and instructed the caravan to get moving. They could not battle the Akkedis without the Suggizon. He had promised Perseus. Besides, he felt they were the perfect race to take over the running of the lizards gem mines.

It was time for them to come out of hiding and for the Akkedis to disappear. He never had any love for the lizard people. They were bad business dealers, greedy and never caring about anyone, not even their own. A selfish nation of creatures that deserved to be vanquished.

The caravan of over a hundred mounted troops set off into the desert, called Saraba. The trek across Saraba is a dangerous one, even for seasoned troops like these.

The heat is relentless, making it almost impossible to travel during daylight, especially when the sun is fully up. The sand worms are a constant threat, with routes having to be plotted that take into account solid rock formations for refuge. This can often double the time it takes to get from one place to another.

Not only are the sand worms a problem, the desert has many tribes, some friendly, others not. Whilst they were well equipped for trouble, they needed to complete this part of their journey with as little distractions as possible.

Qutaybah had ensured there were gifts a plenty to bribe those who could make their passage easier. Arms for some tribes, food for other ones, clothing for another and even gems and gold for some. All would be appeased so this caravan could continue its journey unhindered.

They traveled for almost twelve hours and as they ascended a huge sand dune, an oasis came into view. A small patch of ground with a pool of water and a number of palms that offered shade from the ravages of the midday sun. The caravan headed towards it and in no time, the soldiers and beasts were refreshed by the cool clear liquid. All rested under shade.

"It would be much quicker to go south following the dry river bed, rather than climbing the two huge dunes that stand between us and our destination," Dramand said to Qutaybah.

"Indeed, but I would not wish to go too close to the Akkedis just yet. Besides, we have yet to meet up with the Suggizon. They are crucial to the success of my plan."

Hours of riding had made his back ache, and Qutaybah rubbed at it absentmindedly. "For now, Dramand, enjoy this beautiful oasis. It is the last one on our route. This is my favorite. For some strange reason, a single coconut tree fruits here every time I arrive. No matter what time of year, it always provides me with this refreshing drink of coconut milk. I think it is a magical tree and bears a good omen. I go out of my way to talk to it whenever I am passing."

"Pffff, you talk to a coconut tree?" Dramand scorned good-naturedly.

"Indeed I do. A warrior should always make time for the little things in life. Things that may not seem important, but who knows how anything might change your future, eh?" Qutaybah took a long sip of the drink in the coconut cup.

"Talking to trees, my friend, can only be a sign of desert madness," Dramand warned him. "I fail to see how a coconut tree can be of any use in your life."

"See, it provides me with nutrition, right here in the middle of nowhere, how can that be?"

The debate over the lonely coconut tree, went on well into the night, as the two friends discussed the mundane subject. This eased the strain of travel, as friends are meant to do.

The next day would find them approaching the village that guarded the pass to the Suggizon. Arriving with an army of men would cause consternation, and tensions would be high.

CHAPTER 34

Myriam was restless, as always, though she had not provided blood for a few days. She found she could not sleep in this place. There were no windows to open, no fresh breeze to cool her skin. Just the same stuffy air that kept recycling itself, stale and damp.

Something was bothering her, something niggling at the back of her mind. She had not seen Linz or Hendon for days as the guards had stopped her leaving the room. Luckily she still had the company of her grandmother. Though now she thought about it, the Akkedis had not taken any blood from the Duchess either. That could only mean they were bleeding the young men dry.

With a sudden start she jumped up from her bed. Concern over her companions causing her to pace the floor anxiously. What if they were to go too far and kill Linz and Hendon? She would demand the very next day that she be allowed to see her compatriots. Just as she was composing a speech in her head, she heard a door slowly open. It was the door to the empty room. *Why hadn't they put the boys in there?* she wondered.

As the door opened, she was unsure who to expect, friend or foe. Could it be the Akkedis servant girl, Arriba, whom she had not seen her for a while? Could it be one of the boys, though why would they come that way? All these thoughts quickly scanned through her mind and she felt relief flood over her when she saw the figure move into the light.

"Perseus, it is so good to see you," she said, approaching him. "I was worried you had both been murdered."

"I come with grave news, Queen Myriam." He spoke with a resigned sadness and would not look her in the eye.

Myriam sat down, her legs trembling, readying herself for the bad news.

"Please do not tell me that Ganry is dead?"

When he did not reply, she choked, not wanting to hear those words.

Perseus took her delicate hand, trying to offer some comfort.

"No, but he is close, and there is little I can do," he told her. "That creature, Ghaffar, he tortures him with insects, every day. He puts those vile creatures inside his body and stands there watching as Ganry writhes around in agony. Every day it takes a part of his strength away. If I were to kill Ghaffar, I would be showing my hand too soon. I bring extra food and liquids for Ganry's strength, but even that is helping less and less."

Perseus covered his face with his large hands, rubbing at his skin. It was clear to Myriam that he and Ganry had become close on this expedition. The loss of Ganry would hit him hard.

"Perseus, keep doing all you can for him. I will speak to the others and see if we can come up with some solution. I have a plan, something the Akkedis servant girl let slip about why they drug us before taking the blood. It seems that if we are restful, the blood is of better quality. Well, I think it's time to change all that. We will refuse to co-operate and make them fight for our blood, make things harder, so to speak. That way Ghaffar will need to put his attentions elsewhere, at least for a while."

Perseus did not linger. He wished to hurry back to Ganry and try to ease his wounds. It was his intention to sneak into the medical area and steal some medicines to give him strength. He was not sure they would work on Ganry, as Akkedis physiology is so very different, but anything that might lend Ganry some time would be welcome. He knew there was little hope of Ghaffar holding off the torture, but if he had other urgencies to attend to, as Myriam had planned, then perhaps he could build up Ganry's strength once again.

Myriam stuck to her plan and the next day she made such a fuss at not seeing her two friends, who were only in the room opposite, that the guards had to go and find Ghaffar.

"I will not eat, I refuse to drink, and I hope your Empress dies in agony," she yelled at the Akkedis who brought her breakfast in.

"My dear, whatever is this about?" the Duchess asked as she came into Myriam's room to share breakfast, as they did daily.

"It is time to stop this charade, grandmother. Ganry is in danger and I have not seen Linz or Hendon for days. I will not be treated like this!" Myriam yelled at her grandmother so all the guards could hear her words. Nor did she care if they understood or not, she just needed to get Ghaffar's attention for a few days.

The door was left open and she pushed her way past the guards who seemed unsure of what to do. Moving quickly into the young men's room, she soon saw that they were both sleeping in their cots.

"Wake up, wake up!" she cried. "I want you in my rooms and we will not be parted any more. It is time to lay down a few rules ourselves. Now, boys, wake yourselves, you are needed. I have much to discuss with you."

She pitied them as it was obvious by the darkness of their eyes and the paleness of their skin, that the greedy Akkedis Empress had been feeding from them in large quantities. They needed to be together from now on, protecting one another. Four heads were better than one. It was time to get together and make plans to be free of this dreadful place.

CHAPTER 35

Artas was enjoying his morning ride on his grey dappled horse, Orton. He had not had a moment alone in such a long time. The air was invigorating as the horse cantered along, and they both enjoyed the open space of the meadow. Artas missed being able to do just as he wanted. As Regent everyone seemed to know his every move. He had even refused Lady Leonie joining him on his ride this morning as he simply wanted to be alone.

As they jogged to the top of a steep hill, Artas could see a group of riders moving fast towards him. He could not recognize them from so far away, and decided to keep his distance until he had identified them better. They drew closer and he could now see that one of the riders carried the banner of Qutaybah. Spurring his horse on, he rode down to meet them.

They came to a stop and surrounded him in a circle, eying him warily.

"Do not hinder us," the leader said, sternly, hand hovering over his sword hilt. "We ride for the castle. I have grave news for the Regent."

"That is me, Artas, Regent of Palara. I'd rather hear your message here, away from prying eyes and eaves-droppers."

The leader was a lean man, well muscled with a hardened look about him. He was clearly a veteran of many battles. Always cautious, he looked at the young man before him more closely. His master had described the Regent named Artas to him, and this nobleman fit the description perfectly, even down to the injured leg.

"My name is Jacayb, and I am here with great urgency with regards to your Queen Myriam."

Artas felt a heavy cloud hang over him. This was not what he wanted to hear. Though he was in a rush to know the news, he did not rush the rider who had come so far.

"You have a traitor among your people. He is known as Lord Josiah. That is the only name we have. He is dealing with Ghaffar of the Akkedis to ensure that your Queen does not return," Jacayb finished.

"The Queen still lives then?" Artas asked, hope in his voice.

"Yes, she lives still. As we speak, Qutaybah is rushing to her aid in the Akkedis city. He implores you to send men to help in his mission."

Artas nodded, but said nothing. He turned his horse and led the riders towards the castle.

"Please, you are my guests for as long as you need," he said to Jacayb.

"We can hold up only one night. Then we must return to our own lands for we are needed in battle. Will you be joining us?"

"Alas not me," Artas said, feeling as if he was always the one to miss out on the adventures. "The Queen has appointed me her Regent, so I must deal with Lord Josiah and hold the castle for her until she returns. But, I will be sending our elite troops. You can take a hundred of my best men back with you and I'll send word to the Lakemen. The Chief of the Lakemen is journeying with our Queen, and they will wish to be involved if their Chief is in danger. If you need more, the army of this Kingdom is at your service."

With this news, Jacayb smiled, relieved to have delivered his master's message and to be taking back strong reinforcements. "My master asked only for your best. We do not need numbers, just seasoned soldiers."

"And, my good man, you shall have them at your disposal. I would prefer to take all the army we have to rescue our Queen, but this would not be diplomatic. I shall trust this in the hands of Qutaybah, as I know he is allied to the Duchess and will do all he can to ensure her safety."

The group rode towards the castle and Artas sent the five men to an inn, so that Lord Josiah would not suspect anything should he see them arrive.

When Artas reached his rooms, he called for Leonie and Parsival, informing them of the news he had just received.

Leonie gasped. "I knew he was up to something, but I had not realized his treachery was so deep. What are your intentions for yet another usurper? I could have him disposed of this very evening. My spies have been keeping a close eye on him, and I have reliable men ready to take action at a moment's notice."

The Regent smiled at how prepared and efficient she was. They discussed the implications and possible solutions to dealing with Josiah well into the night.

Artas made his decision the next day.

Lord Josiah was instantly arrested, along with his men that had remained with him. Keeping them all separate, it did not take long for Lady Leonie and her spies to get the right information from them.

She met with the Regent to give him the good news.

"How do you do it, Leonie?" Parsival said, delighted that his Leonie had come on so well. "You are such a delicate creature, that, had I not known it to be true, I would never have believed you to be in charge of spies and torture."

Artas trusted her and knew this intelligence was vital for the banishment of this Lord. Though he would not make the final decision and would leave that up to Myriam.

Until then, Lord Josiah and his loyal men were now imprisoned within the dungeons, all their comforts gone.

CHAPTER 36

The villagers lined up with their weapons, wary that the approaching army were mercenaries. Sampson had been sent for as he was their leader and would know how to deal with these men.

Qutaybah stayed on his camel behind Dramand. He did not want to show himself too soon. First he needed to be certain that a Suggizon still resided in the village. He watched closely as a large man arrived among the villagers and moved out from the throng, making his way towards them.

"What can we do for you?" Sampson asked, giving away no mood whatsoever.

"It is more what we can do you for you, Suggizon," Dramand replied.

An instant murmur buzzed among the villagers. Only few knew that this village was connected to the shape-shifters.

"You have me at an advantage, sir." The leader stood tall and firm, showing no fear just because this man had shown that he knew privileged information. "My name is Sampson, and may I know yours?"

Qutaybah moved from behind Dramand. "I am Qutaybah, a friend of the Suggizon," he said, dismounting from his camel.

Sampson's face lit up with joy as he recognized him. "Qutaybah, my friend, it has been far too long," Sampson said, approaching him. "I thought you had abandoned us, once you knew we were safe."

"Never." Qutaybah laughed as the two large men hugged in friendship. "I come to bring you wealth, as I promised my man, Perseus."

"Perseus still serves you?" Sampson asked, clearly pleased to hear that name. "I also thought my brother had abandoned his family. He is an uncle of three now, whereas there was only one when he left."

The two men parted in their welcoming hug and Sampson turned to the villagers, informing them there was nothing to fear. They began to disperse and go back to their toil.

It was agreed that the mercenaries could camp around the village, and that the residents would make a feast in honor of their guests. The villagers were not short of supplies, and quickly the tables were ladened with food, fine wines and ales.

A celebratory atmosphere was soon thriving and musicians played as a hog was put to roast. The lingering smell of the meat was a welcoming aroma and the soldiers were quick to mingle with the villagers, enjoying their welcoming hospitality.

Qutaybah was taken to Sampson's house where they could talk further in peace and quiet.

"Thank you for such a welcome," Qutaybah thanked Sampson. "The trek across the desert is a difficult one, ladened with dangers. This will help the men relax."

"Why have you come so far?" Sampson questioned. "I fear it must only be with grave news." A frown knitted in his brow.

"We are here to liberate the gem mines that the Akkedis so jealously guard. We wish to drive them out of this land. I feel it only right that your people, together with my guidance, should rule in their place," Qutaybah explained, accepting a mug of beer from a pretty girl.

"We have grown greatly in numbers, all thanks to you, Qutaybah." Sampson clinked his tankard on his companions, in a toast of this good news. "As always agreed, our people are at your disposal. It seems that yet again you offer us a new life, a new opportunity, one I believe we are just about ready for. At the moment we are surviving, getting by, but the gems will help feed our children and build an army to keep those away that wish us harm. Again, my friend, you honor us with hope."

"We have to do this as discretely as possible. We do not want to attract any unwanted attention. Once your people are firmly installed in place, I feel we could rebuff any attempts to take from us what is rightfully yours. Until then, we need to be cautious," Qutaybah said. "I also have another personal problem to resolve with the Akkedis Empress, but that does not need to involve you, though Perseus is helping me with that matter."

"Anything that my brother deems important is also important to his people. We will help with your personal matter also. But tonight, we must celebrate your return. You are the one to save our race from extinction. You will always hold a place of honor within our community. Please, let us go join in the celebrations, and tomorrow I will go personally to our city and bring back forces."

"A city now, eh?" Qutaybah questioned, surprised they had grown so quickly.

"We breed constantly," Sampson smiled at providing this information. "From the ravaged population that you rescued, we are now thriving in numbers. Most of our people are young, but they are taught the importance of survival. Fighting is now our utmost priority, as well as breeding, of course."

Qutaybah laughed, he had always liked the sense of humor of the Suggizon. They had struggled for survival and this had made them appreciate life all the more. He considered himself lucky to have known them. Even more, he was glad to have made them his allies. With the right situation, they will be a formidable race and the perfect partners for attacking the Akkedis with whom they had a personal quarrel.

There was no love lost between the Akkedis and the Suggizon. It was the Akkedis that had brought about their downfall. They were once a powerful race in Vandemland, and a union between their races was arranged through a marriage. The Akkedis Empress' daughter and one of the Suggizon princes were to make this bond. But the union was a trick, its purpose to allow the Akkedis to rule the Suggizon and take their lands.

In the resulting battles many of the princes' people were killed, which devastated their population. Some revenge was extracted when the Suggizon prince managed to kill his Akkedis wife.

To compound matters further, certain tribes in Vandemland saw the Suggizon as a delicacy when in snake form, and a thriving black market trade had grown in selling their flesh. The Akkedis promoted this, even trading Suggizon slaves on the black market. The Suggizon people would welcome the opportunity to avenge their kind.

CHAPTER 37

Ghaffar knew that the only way to move the young male humans was going to be by force, and he had hoped to avoid that, just yet. There would time enough to cause plenty of discomfort for these annoying humans soon. He was surprised just how compliant the human Queen had been, and the quality of her blood had been excellent. He would not want to jeopardize that. He might as well go along with their demands.

Just as he was about to go to the dungeon and observe the human Ganry being tortured with the kewers, he had been called upon. This annoyed him, as it gave him great pleasure to watch this strong human cry out in such pain, each day he was weakening.

It would be easy to simply allow Sileta to instruct the insects to finish him, but where was the fun in that. It would be over in seconds. This way he got to see a human in agony for hours, every single day. It was very satisfying.

Today though, he had been called away from his preferred entertainment. The human Queen was refusing admittance into her room, and she was holding all the other humans in there with her. Her demands were easy enough to comply with. She simply requested that the young male humans be put in the adjoining room to hers instead of the the one opposite. She wanted the humans to be together. Of course, he would refuse to start with. He needed to make them suffer his wrath first.

"My lady, just open up your door so we can discuss this in a more reasonable manner," Ghaffar said.

"I am not opening this door until you guarantee that I can see Ganry," Myriam shouted back at him. "You can fight for your blood, Akkedis traitor, because it will not be provided voluntarily any more."

"Do you think this wise?" Hendon asked of Myriam, unsure of her motives in causing this commotion.

"I'm only playing for time," she explained to Hendon and Linz. They both looked completely exhausted and she felt she had taken this action just in time. "We must think of a way to stop the torture that Ghaffar does to Ganry with those disgusting insects. He puts him through agony on a daily basis and I have to do something. Perseus came to tell me that Ganry will not last out much longer."

"My granddaughter speaks the truth," the Duchess joined in. "Once Ganry and Perseus are dead, you two shall be next. We will be saved until last because the Akkedis Empress needs the strength supplied within our blood. It is time for us to make our first stand, if only to delay things."

"Now I understand my dream last night," Hendon told them. "Barnaby showed me a tiny worm which he said is a deadly predator of the beetle. I did not know why he was telling me this, but it all makes sense now. I do wish he would not communicate in riddles."

"This is good news, indeed!" Myriam proclaimed, her heart lightened at the thought that Ganry could yet be saved.

"The keeper of the kewers will have a number of these worms as they are needed to control the blood sucking insects used on Ganry," Hendon explained. "Do you think that Perseus could manage to get some?"

"He is to come to me this very evening. We can speak to him and tell him what to look for. This will begin our rebellion, even if it gets us nowhere."

"Fear not, my granddaughter, we only have to delay things for a short while," her grandmother said. "Plus, we need to do all we can to make sure we all stay alive, including Ganry and Perseus."

All had gone quiet in the corridor, but Myriam's door and all the other doors to the adjoining rooms remained locked from the inside. They were not allowing the Akkedis in, and they would have to physically break down the doors. Myriam knew she would need to relent soon, but for this day and night, the Akkedis could remain outside of their rooms.

Ghaffar made his way slowly to report to his Empress, a meeting he was not looking forward to. She will be furious that he is empty handed of her food. He'll need to calm her and assure her that this situation is only temporary, and all will be back to normal the very next day.

Ghaffar knew that this supply could not last forever, but for now, he simply needed to make these humans go back to allowing their blood to be taken. It would be so much harder should they need to be forced. The power of the red juice would not be the same if the humans were put under duress. He must go back to the human Queen and agree to her demands, if that is what it was going to take.

He returned and knocked upon Queen Myriam's door, promising to listen to all she had to say.

CHAPTER 38

Parsival had agreed to lead the elite force that was to venture into Vandemland to help free Queen Myriam. It had been arranged for him to meet with the Lakemen at the border. Jacayb, Qutaybah's man, had shown him their secret way to get through the border with little danger, and then he had drawn a map of the route to the Akkedis city.

He sat alone now in his small camp, awaiting the arrival of Linz's tribe. They would only send the best to save their Chief, so he was confident that he would be guiding a group of brave warriors.

Parsival was surprised when Artas had asked him to lead the rescue party, but he had willingly accepted. The Kingdom of Palara had suffered much over the last few years from the usurper Harald. It needed its right and proper Queen returned to the throne.

Whilst he waited he reflected on the moment he and Lady Leonie had attempted to assassinate Duke Harald, the old king's brother. A failed attempt that almost cost them their lives. Harald had murdered the king, and most of his loyal followers, so he could become Regent. Only Princess Myriam, the rightful heir, was stopping him from becoming a king. Eventually, many other nobles rose against him and he was overthrown and killed in battle, leaving Myriam as Queen.

They had thought their troubles to be ended, at least for a while, but alas not. Again the royal family of Palara were in trouble. He was fond of Queen Myriam and felt she would do much good for the Kingdom.

When she had insisted in participating on a quest to save her grandmother, the Duchess of D'Anjue, who had withstood Harald's torturers by refusing to reveal Myriam's whereabouts, he understood her loyalty. At first no one knew what had happened to the Duchess. It was a great relief when they discovered she had been saved by Ghaffar, but it soon became clear that she was not safe.

Recently, Regent Artas had received word that Myriam, her grandmother, Chief Linz of the Lake people and Hendon, a forest dweller, had all become prisoners of the Akkedis. Artas had organized their rescue, immediately, and had tasked Parsival with leading the mission, a role that Artas would have preferred to have taken himself. Alas this could not be though because Myriam had left him in charge as Regent, and that meant he had to stay in the kingdom.

Parsival had become good friends with Artas, and he worried how he would fare in his absence. Knowing that Lady Leonie remained a close adviser, helped. The three of them had become quite a team running the kingdom while Queen Myriam was away. They were all loyal to the Queen and each would give up their lives to save her.

As Parsival sat in the darkness, pondering over his present situation, a large hand grabbed at his mouth and a strong arm around his throat. Believing he had been taken by bandits, he feared he may not be able to do Artas's work after all, as surely this must mean his death. Bandits on the borders were notoriously evil, killing anyone they could steal from.

Someone kneeled in front of him and spoke, but he could not understand the dialect. He wished he had paid more attention in his younger days in lessons of other languages. Then the male voice spoke in his Queen's language.

"Are you Parsival?" the voice asked.

He nodded his head, relief flooding his emotions.

"We could not be sure, but we meant no harm," the lake man said to him, apologetically.

They were well known for their lack of etiquette, having been separate from the rest of Palara for a long time. They still needed much adjustment in their social skills. Though he had met their Chief, Linz, who was much more civilized in his behavior.

"No matter," Parsival said, rubbing at his throat from the heavy handed soldier who had nearly throttled him. "We must continue our journey immediately, as we need to get through the border by dawn. He knew they would have traveled hard already to have got here so quickly, but it was important that they cover as much ground as possible before they rested.

It was agreed and they set off at once. The lake people were experienced at keeping themselves unseen, in a world that did not even know of their existence. It was Princess Myriam who had discovered them in her travels to escape Duke Harald.

"First we will travel on foot," Parsival told the leader. "There are camels awaiting us in Vandemland to help us traverse the desert. We need to avoid being followed. To do this we need to blend in and dress as Vandemlanders. I have the funds to purchase the required clothing for your men. Are you agreeable to this?"

"For our Chief, we will do everything for his safety," the leader replied.

"Good. Then let us get started. We have a long journey ahead and the lives of our leaders may very well depend on our haste."

CHAPTER 39

When Perseus arrived later that night, Hendon took him aside and instructed him on what he needed. Perseus was happy to help in any way he could, as he could see that Ganry was deteriorating every day.

"Hendon, how does Barnaby say this will work?" Myriam asked him, wondering if Barnaby was a figment of Hendon's imagination.

"It's a natural predator of the insects that they are using to torture Ganry," Hendon described. "It will need to be inserted into Ganry's body and it will attack and kill the kewers. It will not harm Ganry in any way, or so Barnaby promises me."

"Are you certain about this, Hendon? Placing a live bug into a weakened Ganry, will it be safe?" Myriam questioned him further. She feared for her protector and would not want to do anything that might harm him.

"It is no bigger than my smallest finger nail, so I hardly think it can hurt Ganry any more than he's already being hurt. The kewers are bigger, from what

Perseus tells us. We need to act quickly. Ganry is to swallow the creature, and it spits out a deadly silk at the kewers. Eventually, it will leave the host as it cannot feed in the human body."

Perseus left immediately to try and obtain the worm that Hendon had described, leaving the others to discuss their own plan of action.

"We cannot hold off Ghaffar any longer," Myriam said. "Yesterday, I agreed to allow the food in and asked for one more day of rest. Today, when I met with him, I had to agree that all could go back to normal so long as you and Linz can stay in the room that adjoins mine, where Ganry stayed. I feel so much safer knowing we can all contact each other. Though it may all be in vain. The Lizard Empress is determined to drain us dry."

The Duchess came to Myriam's side and hugged her. "My dear, you are doing all that you can, and your delaying tactics will prove useful. They will be here soon, I know it."

"Grandmother, I appreciate your optimism, but how can Qutaybah infiltrate an entire city of Akkedis? It would take a large army, and that would need the permission of the King of Vandemland. I doubt even he would allow a whole race to be attacked."

"The King of Vandemland is a fool," Duchess D'Anjue announced. "If he were to find out that you were prisoner here, he would probably invade your kingdom while you were away. All he cares about are his taxes, and I would imagine that Empress Gishja pays more than her fair share. The King of Vandemland would not wish to antagonize her for fear of losing income."

Linz had said very little throughout the lock-in. He felt that the last blood collecting session had made him very weary. His body would not take many more sessions, but he did not wish to tell anyone as they had their own worries. He was sad for his people, as this would mean they would have lost two chief's, very close together.

They had gained so much with Queen Myriam. Their own land, freedom to show themselves and feel safe. Yet, that could all be taken away if she were to die here. Feeling so useless that he could not save her, he felt shame at his weakness.

How could he return to his people and take his rightful place as a chief? He was never strong enough for that role. With his friend, Wyatt, by his side, he had felt capable, but since his death he felt lost and alone. The sad loss of his trainer and friend had been hard to accept, and now he felt that death might be a welcome end.

"You must have faith," he heard Hendon say to him, as if he was reading his mind. "Linz, you must believe that we are going to get away from this place."

"I would like to believe that I played a part in our rescue, but this will not be," Linz replied, feeling utterly miserable. "I don't even fear those ugly creatures any more. Let the Rooggaru take me, I will injure it as it finishes me off."

The adjoining door squeaked as it opened, and surprisingly, Perseus entered the room. Linz rose in greeting, but his weakened legs buckled under the strain and he almost collapsed to the floor. Hendon was soon at hand and helped his friend to sit back down.

"You do well to rest, for now, young Chief," Perseus said, approaching him. "Soon your strength will return and you will have your revenge on the Akkedis."

Linz doubted such words. "I will die in this place," he said to Perseus.

"No, Chief Linz, you will not." Perseus gave him soothing words. "You only need to be strong for a little while longer, trust me."

"Linz is not himself," Myriam explained to Perseus. "I think we are all weakening, and the thought of Ganry leaving us unprotected gives us nothing but sadness."

"Perseus," Hendon said, "you have returned quicker than I expected. Have you located the creature?"

"I have it here." Perseus took a small wooden box from his pocket and passed it to Hendon.

Hendon carefully opened the box and peered inside. There was a small white worm curling up at the bottom of the box, trying to avoid the light. It was mostly white, but its back glinted with a hint of grey. It looked too small to do anything any harm.

"You're never going to put that inside of Ganry?" Myriam gasped, looking at the slimy worm over Hendon's shoulder.

"This will save him, Barnaby assures me. Besides," Hendon continued, pessimistically, "what other choices do we have?"

He handed the box back to Perseus. Perseus took the box and looked at Hendon with misgivings.

"Have faith," Hendon said, hoping that Perseus would not let him down. "Ganry must swallow it as it needs to get into his system. Promise me you will deliver it to him, and stress the urgency?"

Perseus nodded his head and left the room, leaving the party to watch after him and wonder how this would all end.

CHAPTER 40

When Sampson returned from the city of the Suggizon, he came with a troop of thirty soldiers. These were fine men and women, well trained in the art of combat. Qutaybah's confidence rose as he studied them. They were all fine Suggizon specimens and appeared strong and healthy.

"If this is an example of your nation, then you are ready to face the world head on and take your rightful place back in society," Qutaybah said to Sampson.

"Thank you, we are indeed ready to take our rightful place back again. We are a good and gentle people, but we will act with the utmost violence against those who would mean us harm. We learned much from our previous encounter with the Akkedis. Though our leaders do not condone the annihilation of the lizards, they are prepared to help save your allies. I am instructed only to take control of the mines but to spare the Akkedis, banish them if necessary, or offer them work. We are not

187

prepared to commit genocide and annihilate another race. We have come too close to that ourselves."

Qutaybah bowed his head in respect. He could understand why the Suggizon felt this way, but Qutaybah did not agree. The Empress of the Akkedis had made a mistake in threatening those that were close to him, a mistake she would soon regret. Long enough had the Akkedis owned the gem mines and become a greedy people. It was time to share out their spoils and for them to find another land to live in. Despite Sampson's desire, he would see that the Akkedis Empress would die, and that the Akkedis people were driven out.

He looked upon the thirty Suggizon that would be following his lead, and he felt good that his force was made up of different races. Yesterday, Jacayb had sent word that he had arrived at the agreed meeting point with one hundred Palarian soldiers, and another fifty Lakemen had joined him there.

The Akkedis would have more in numbers, but Qutaybah would have the element of surprise and well trained elite fighters. His spies had told him that the Akkedis soldiers were demoralized and unprepared to fight. Much discontent was in the Akkedis camp with many turning to drink and drugs and no order whatsoever. All of this was an advantage to Qutaybah and his force. Of course the death of the Empress was of the utmost importance, but all he could do was pray that Perseus could succeed with the task set before him.

The next day saw Qutaybah leaving behind the small village and taking his army across the desert. For now, they would be safe, as the this part of Vandemland was uninhabitable. Soon they would come across areas where the nomadic tribes wandered. He was not concerned about them. He was friendly with most of their leaders, but they needed to stay away from the cities and any area that the King's army patrolled.

Should the King discover Qutaybah's plans, he would not be pleased. Yet once victory was achieved, the King would care little on who ruled the mines, so long as the taxes were paid as usual.

Parsival had found his way to the meeting point using the map that was provided by Jacayb. Once there, they laid low for a while, waiting the arrival of the mercenaries. He did not have long to wait and soon Jacayb arrived with his men.

Jacayb led them to a set of caves, and here they would hide until the arrival of Qutaybah. There were food supplies aplenty, already stored within the chambers of this subterranean system. Plus an underground river that helped with the bathing of soldiers.

"Will we be traveling a long way once the rest of the army arrives?" Parsival was curious how far they had to go to get to this elusive lizard city.

"Some will travel within the tunnels, and some will go in the secret entrance, but all will arrive at the underground city ready for battle," Jacayb explained. "We will keep the camels herded here for when we are done."

The news of an underground city surprised Parsival, but the more he thought about it, the more it made sense. He kept his thoughts to himself. He did not wish the men to be openly discussing the inevitable battle. They were presently enjoying the rest and relaxation after days of hard trekking. The fighting would be here all too soon, so it was good that they had other things to occupy their minds.

CHAPTER 41

Perseus had freed Ganry from his shackles as he had done every day since they had been captured, but it helped less and less. The muscular warrior was truly exhausted from his daily torture of those insects that drained him.

Perseus looked forward to receiving the sign that his master was close and he could kill the Akkedis Empress, exacting his revenge on these lizards. Ghaffar would be one of the first to die. He would take great pleasure in this, for all the pain he had caused, not only for Ganry, but for the Queen and her family. Qutaybah had stressed to him that not only was he to kill the Lizard Empress, but he was also there to protect the Duchess and her family.

Perseus liked his master. He was fair and treated him with respect. He knew that though there was personal gain for Qutaybah in this, it was also for the benefit of the Suggizon nation, to help them progress in a world that had given them up for dead.

He put Ganry's head on his lap and slowly fed him water.

"Come, my friend, it is nearly over and I need your strength once more," Perseus said.

"You mean I'm nearly dead?" Ganry managed to grumble, in a deep hoarse voice. "Hah. If you think I'm helping you when I'm a ghost, you can think again, you snake slithering, sneaky..." his words were interrupted as his body was wracked with a deep chesty coughing. Blood spots appeared on the hand that he covered his mouth with.

"Save your strength." Perseus ignored Ganry's insults. "Hendon has sent you a life saving gift." He opened up his hand to show Ganry a strange creature that scuttled about on his palm.

"And what do I do with that, eat it?" Ganry meant his words as a joke, but one look at Perseus's face told him that was exactly what he had to do.

"Are you mad, Perseus? Do I not suffer enough with the creatures that odious little man puts into my body, you want me to take another? Please, just leave me to die."

"I need you, Ganry, and your Queen needs you. Once we are free of this place then you are welcome to die as you wish. Stop feeling sorry for yourself and take this creature. This is not going to be easy, but you must swallow it with this water."

Ganry waved his had in one movement, indicating this was all nonsense. "What manner of magic is this meant to be then?" he asked, with no faith whatsoever in Hendon's gift.

"Hendon assures me that this creature will kill the insects that Ghaffar tortures you with. You must trust me, and trust Hendon. Your Queen commands it of you."

"My daughter was just as bossy as Myriam, do you know that?" Ganry was feverish and probably hallucinating. "These women, they tell us what to do our whole lives, as sisters and daughters, as mothers and as wives."

"Put this on your tongue," Perseus instructed the rambling warrior. "Now swallow a whole cup of water to wash it down," he said, tipping the clay cup between Ganry's lips. "Is it gone yet?"

"Is what gone?" Ganry questioned, unsure where he was as he sweated hot and shivered cold. These days he could not remember very much. He seemed to think his daughter was in danger but he could not remember why.

Perseus put Ganry back into his shackles so he hung from the cave wall. Putting himself back into his own chains, just in time, he heard the lock turning and in walked Ghaffar.

"Greetings," he said in a jolly voice as he entered the room, with the female Sileta following him through the door. "How you must have missed me yesterday, but I had other important appointments. However, today I thought we would finish our little game. Sileta here will be placing every single one of her lovely pets inside of your body, Ganry, and then we shall say our goodbyes. It has been fun while it lasted, but now I must concentrate my mind on other matters."

Ganry could hear talking, in the distance, but he could make no sense of the words. His mind was whirring, someone was in danger, someone close to him, but he could not quite grasp who it was.

A shiver ran through his body as a strange woman stood in front of him. She looked odd, shimmering, her skin seemed to crawl. Somewhere in his mind he realized that she was covered in insects, and soon those insects would be inside him, tormenting him until he could take it no more.

He tried to squirm his body away from her as she approached him. He felt, rather than saw the insects, as they burrowed into his skin causing him to cry out in pain.

Over the days of torture, Ghaffar had instructed Sileta not to let the insects close to Ganry's heart. Instead he wanted Ganry to suffer in agonizing pain as he slowly died. He enjoyed seeing him squirm and scream as the insects burrowed through his body. Long ago was the pretense of torturing him for information done away with. But today it was time to end the fun.

"Let us finish him, Sileta," Ghaffar said with finality. "Let your creatures have the prize they so desire, while it still barely beats."

Sileta murmured some words that Ganry could not comprehend. Gently she rubbed her hands along his torso. Ganry could feel little tremors where she touched him. Those tremors gave the kewers their entry point. In a frenzy they made their way to the victim's heart.

It was not just the kewers that felt the tremors, unbeknown to Ghaffar and Sileta, the insects were already dying as quickly as they entered. The tremors alerted the creature that Ganry had swallowed, and it was squirming around his blood stream, shooting out its acid silk and killing the kewers at a very fast rate.

Sileta faltered and pulled her hands away from Ganry. She screamed out, as if in terrible pain.

"Quickly, instruct them to go to the heart," Ghaffar shouted at her, worried something was amiss.

"I cannot," she cried out, falling onto the floor and curling up in a ball as if in agony. "My pets are dying, what is he doing to them?" she screamed, before passing out unconscious on the hard stone floor.

Ganry became aware of a woman falling down. He stared at a small man, or what resembled a man, but he was not sure if it was really human. His skin seemed to shift before his eyes, one moment it was smooth and then it appeared hard and scaly.

As each kewer was killed within him, his own strength returned. He felt a power coursing through him, invigorating him. Suddenly, he was conscious of his shackles, and he pulled on them, straining at them with his revitalized muscles. He had to escape these bonds, his daughter, nay, his Queen needed him.

At that moment, Perseus changed into a giant snake, falling free from his shackles and slithering straight towards Ghaffar. The little lizard man stood shaking, shock written on his features as he watched the events unfold before him.

All control was gone. The female, Sileta, looked dead. The human, Ganry, who only moments ago looked close to death, was now seemingly full of strength. But worse, what he thought was a human, Perseus, was in fact one of those dreaded Suggizon creatures, and it was heading towards him with malice in its eyes.

Ghaffar's survival instincts took over, and he found his feet. He pushed the guard behind him out of his way and into the path of the advancing Suggizon. Perseus lunged at the escaping Ghaffar but the guard blocked his way.

Ghaffar was quickly out of the door and heading deep into the caves. He knew these tunnels better than any other and he soon made his escape. Should he run to the Empress and let her know that she was in danger? Perhaps, but for a short while he would do better to hide. Who knows what calamity might be in these corridors, now that sickening creature was loose? He doubted there was more than one of them. It may be advantageous to stay hidden and make his escape when the commotion stopped.

CHAPTER 42

Myriam, in exchange for allowing Linz and Hendon to occupy the adjoining empty room, had promised Ghaffar she would provide double quantity of her blood. She wanted them close, but also their room was how Perseus came to them, from a tunnel under one of the beds. She felt it safer, with less chance of being discovered if they occupied the room. They had only recently finished taking her blood and she was exhausted. She hoped that Empress Gishja choked on it.

A loud noise coming from the boy's room startled her. She did not have the strength to go and investigate. Instead she waited patiently, knowing the commotion would come to her eventually. And, it did exactly that, but it was not from the room that events started to unfold.

The main door leading out to the corridor flew open. It was Arriba, looking disheveled and distressed.

"Queen Myriam, your man has escaped and he has freed me too. Ghaffar had me locked away because he suspected that I'd helped you." Arriba came into the room and fell at Myriam's feet. "Now, my lady, I want to help you get away from here and back to your own people. It is wrong what we have done."

"Oh, Arriba, I'm so glad they haven't harmed you, I was worried and…"

Linz suddenly burst through the adjoining door and into Myriam's room, interrupting her reply to the Akkedis female. He looked excited and agitated, all at once.

"Myriam, look, it has begun…" he moved aside to allow the person behind him to enter her room.

"Ganry!" Myriam cried. She found the strength to stand and greet him. "Oh Ganry, I have so missed you. What is happening?"

Ganry stepped into the room and Perseus quickly followed him. He had changed back into his human form.

"My Queen, thanks to my friends, I have survived the torture of that odious little man and I am here to help. But we must act quickly," Ganry replied.

He turned to Linz and Hendon. "You two, quickly, block all the doorways that lead to the passageways. Every piece of furniture needs to be used in making a barrier. Here, we will finally make our stand."

Linz and Hendon got to work instantly, with the help of Perseus, all furniture was pushed and carried to block the three doorways, one in each room.

"I trust you have a plan, Perseus?" the Duchess questioned.

"My only plan was to save Ganry," he replied as he moved the last piece of heavy furniture in front of Myriam's door. "I have not yet had a sign from my master, but I sense my people are not far. This could mean that they are in the tunnels. I am going to make my way to the outer tunnels and see if I can find out more. Once I'm sure that Qutaybah is here, I will make my move to the Akkedis Empress."

"She is a fierce foe," the Duchess replied. "You should not take her on alone."

"He is not alone, Duchess," Ganry joined the conversation. "I will have his back."

"And I," Linz added. "It is time we drew some blood of our own."

"I fear even with you three warriors, she will be difficult to overcome. She has just fed from the strongest of royal blood," the Duchess reminded them.

"She is not as strong as she used to be," Hendon said. "She is old and much weakened. I feel our blood does not increase her strength, but only allows her to live."

"Let us hope so," Perseus said, patting Hendon on the shoulders in encouragement. "I go now. I must search the outer tunnels. I will return in a few hours."

"Ghaffar fled in terror of his life," Ganry told them. "Somehow, I doubt he'll go to his Empress with such dire news of our escape. This may give us a slight advantage, for while she is unaware of what has happened, we can stay ahead of the game. My fingers are itching for revenge."

Perseus changed into his snake form in front of them. Only Arriba shrunk back in fear. The others all knew this creature was not a danger to them. He quickly left by the tunnel under the bed.

"I must leave," Arriba said to the humans, realizing the dangers of her being found in the room with them. Should she be discovered here, this would surely lead to her death.

"What will they do to you though, Arriba, when they find out you have escaped?"

"It will not matter because Ghaffar is the one who was punishing me. If he is in hiding, then I will be safe. It is better this way. I may find a way to help you by being among my own people. I will watch closely and do all I can to delay your capture and help with your escape. But I cannot stay here and be seen as a traitor to my people."

"Of course, you are quite right, child," the Duchess was the first to agree. "She can help us far better from the outside. Let us get her out of these rooms. I suggest she goes through the tunnel that Perseus has left. That way she will escape the attention of the guards."

Arriba stepped into the adjoining room with Linz and Hendon, staring at the tunnel with a good deal of apprehension. She knew that this was where the Suggizon had gone. She had always been told, from being a young child, that the snake creatures were their mortal enemies. Evil monsters that fed on the babies of the Akkedis. This one did not seem like that. It was friendly, and these humans trusted it. Arriba was beginning to think a lot of what she had been taught was wrong.

Linz and Hendon helped her climb down the tunnel. None knew where it would take her, but she was willing to risk this. She knew she could help the humans better if she were to mingle with her own kind. There was nothing she could do to help if she stayed here, cowering from Ghaffar. Myriam grabbed a hold of her hand before she disappeared down the tunnel. "Thank you, Arriba. Even if you cannot help, I thank you for being a friend."

Arriba just nodded her head. She had every intention on helping, somehow. She did not wish to hurt her Empress, but she hated Ghaffar and would gladly see his reign end.

Arriba followed the narrow passageway, hoping it did not collapse on her, though it looked well used. Perseus must have been visiting with the humans for some time now.

Finally, she came to its end and breathed a sigh of relief to find herself in a wine cellar. A large empty barrel covered the hole to the tunnel. She moved it aside and climbed out of the hole, making sure to replace the barrel before leaving the cellar. It would be a good way for the humans to leave their rooms, when the time was right.

For now, she needed to find out what was happening. Did her Empress know of this incident yet? Had Ghaffar come out of hiding?

A female Akkedis left the wine cellar carrying a barrel of ale. This was not an unusual sight, and no one noticed her. The bar was full of male Akkedis, gambling and shouting loudly at the tables. None noticed Arriba leaving the inn. She had placed her barrel by the bar and simply walked out onto the streets of the Akkedis underground city. There she would try and find help for the imprisoned human Queen and her comrades. She felt she owed them that, at least.

CHAPTER 43

Qutaybah had taken the humans, on foot, towards the tunnels that enter the Akkedis city. He had a contact that was to show them a way that they could enter the city unnoticed. The treacherous guard would also get word to Perseus to begin his own battle within the city.

Jacayb was the only one to approach the entrance, so he could meet the contact who was guarding on the outer perimeter of the city. He had no idea what Qutaybah had promised this individual, but he was surprised that such a large Akkedis would betray his own Empress.

He knew that Akkedis were a greedy people and in most cases everyone had their price, but he was still surprised at his betrayal. The Akkedis guard passed him a map that they were to follow. When he returned to the human soldiers who were hiding behind rocky crags, Jacayb told Qutaybah that he did not trust the Akkedis, fearing this could be a trap.

"Not for what I'm paying him, believe me," Qutaybah tried to reassure Jacayb. "He is well and truly bought. He is a greedy swine who cares only about his own self."

The Suggizon changed into their snake form and dug through the underground tunnels. They would enter the city first. Sampson was in the lead, and hoped to find his brother, Perseus. They did not need a map as they could sense their way through the ground and knew exactly where they were tunneling to.

It did not take them long to enter the city, arriving under a bridge that crossed over a large underground river. They stayed within their own tunnel network, making their way around the city, so that when the humans arrived they were ready to attack from the inside.

Perseus felt it. He knew that not only were his people close at hand, but also was his brother. Qutaybah had kept his part of the bargain, bringing in his brethren to share in the spoils. Now everything was in motion and taking down the Akkedis Empress was his first priority.

Before meeting with his people, he would first return to the humans and help them out of the chambers they were imprisoned within. He knew that Ganry would want to be by his side when he confronts the Empress Gishja.

The entrance for the humans was through the waterways that led into the city. The stench was appalling. All the men waded ankle deep in the water rushing through the tunnels, which emptied into an underground river.

Despite the stench, Parsival was impressed with the clever plumbing. At least it proved the Akkedis were not all fools. Parsival placed his hand on the hilt of his sword, expecting any moment to come across the lizards.

It turned out that they had a long walk as the entrance was some way from the inner city. As they walked the narrow tunnels, they could tell they were getting deeper underground. The air grew thicker and staler until it was almost unbreathable. Yet, every now and then, an outlet allowed a rush of fresh air. It seemed that the Akkedis had built a ventilation system, again proving that they were not all simple.

The troops marched onwards, eventually arriving at a large wooden gateway. At the other side of the gate flowed an underground river. This could prove a great difficulty, as not all the men would be capable of swimming.

Qutaybah made his way to the front of the men to inspect the gate. He was glad he had done so as he spotted a man in a boat, waving over to them. He instantly recognized the man as a Suggizon. The boat, leading other boats, made its way over to the gateway.

"We sensed your arrival," the Suggizon said. "We are spread throughout the city and will take your men to the strategic points. Sampson awaits you eagerly. He only needs your word and we go in to attack."

"We are fortunate that you have managed to organize yourselves so quickly," Qutaybah said to the Suggizon, who helped him into the awaiting boat as it bobbed up and down on the river's flow. "I knew your people would naturally fit into this environment, and I was right. I think this place was built just for you, and you will thrive and prosper here."

CHAPTER 44

Perseus quickly made his way back to the chambers where his companions were held. He arrived through the tunnel to find them armed with the swords he had provided earlier, and ready for battle. The Akkedis guards were furiously banging on the doors trying to gain entry.

"Ganry," Perseus called out, "it is time for you all to move before the guards break down that door. My master has arrived, and his attack is imminent."

Linz and Hendon stood with sword and staff, respectively, ready to confront the attacking Akkedis at the other side of the door. The young men grinned, neither of them were seasoned warriors but they were both keen to be free of this place and mete out some justice on the treacherous Akkedis.

"The tunnel is ready. I have secured it so we can all pass through safely. Come, Ganry, you should go first with your sword at the ready, followed by the Queen and the Duchess," he suggested to Queen Myriam's protector.

"This is it. The battle is upon us and our friend here has not let us down." Ganry placed his hand upon Perseus's strong shoulders.

"I thank you, Perseus," Myriam said to him directly. "For all that you have done for us."

"I would not let Ganry miss the Akkedis Empress' death. He would never forgive me." Perseus grinned back at big seasoned warrior.

Within moments they each crawled down the narrow tunnel that Perseus had been using as his entrance. He had made it wider each time and more secure. Although it was still a tight fit for most of them, it was passable. They emerged in what appeared to be a wine cellar, and there they found Arriba.

"I was just coming back for the Queen and Duchess," she said. "I have a safe place for them to take refuge. Will you trust me?" she asked them.

"My dear," the Duchess was the one to reply, "of course we do. You have a good heart and you have our friendship."

In the distance, the sounds of battle could be heard. Now they knew for certain that the attack had started on the city. Arriba silently crept into the bar. Luckily it was empty, as all the Akkedis were in the street investigating the commotion. No Akkedis male likes to miss out on a street brawl.

"Quickly, now is the time to flee. Do you men have a strategy?" Arriba asked of Ganry.

"Indeed we do, and thank you Arriba, for taking care of our Queen," Ganry replied.

Arriba bowed her head slightly in acceptance, watching as the male humans fled the inn. She grabbed the wrists of each female and they fled also, though in a different direction.

"We cannot stay in the streets for too long," Arriba said as they moved quickly through the streets of the city. "The Akkedis are suspicious and will notice you sooner or later. My hiding place is in a public location, but there is a part of it that you can hide in safely."

Arriba led them quietly through the streets, occasionally stopping to take cover from the Akkedis soldiers that passed close by. Eventually they reached a large building and Arriba took them to the rear, where they entered in through a back door.

Myriam stood admiring the grand building and mused that in better times she would love to study the Akkedis architecture, when suddenly and unceremoniously, her arm was yanked and she was dragged further into the building.

"Sorry, my Lady," Arriba apologized, "but we must keep moving. It is not safe for you near the streets."

Myriam merely nodded her understanding and followed after Arriba, who led them through a procession of corridors and then down a number of stone stairways.

"This is our public library, the best loved municipal building. We Akkedis love to read. You will be in the basement where there is a tunnel that leads to an underground river," Arriba explained, panting as she spoke.

"There is an underground river in the middle of the desert?" Myriam questioned.

"Yes. Our city is built on it. This river has provided us with water for hundreds of years. Without it we would not be able to stay here."

Arriba took them deeper and deeper into the earth, and soon they could hear the river. She opened up a wooden door and led them into a large chamber, lighting the sconces on the wall.

"This room is a few feet above the river, but still remains dry," Arriba told them. "I have chosen it as it is not in use."

"Will you be staying with us, Arriba?" Myriam asked.

"If you wish, my Lady, but for now I must go get some supplies. Please stay here and keep quiet. I will return soon with bedding and food, but this is as safe a place as any."

With those words Arriba was gone and the female humans were left alone.

CHAPTER 45

The streets of the Akkedis city were filled with the sounds of clashing swords as Qutaybah's men fought with the defending Akkedis soldiers. Most Akkedis males had run into the streets to join the battle and defend their city. What the Akkedis citizens confronted turned their blood to ice. Engaged in battle with their army were the Suggizon, huge snake like creatures, the sworn enemy of the Akkedis.

The battle was in full flow and the advancing humans and Suggizon were making progress into the city. Sampson was leading a party of his own people, some in their human form and others changed into snakes. It was the snake form that inspired most fear in the Akkedis. Many fled at the sheer sight of them, only to be run down as the giant snakes wrapped themselves around their thick skinned bodies, crushing them until they breathed no more. Many were brave and stood their ground, only to be slaughtered by the sharp blades of the warriors or the slow constricting death of the snakes.

Sampson spotted a small group of Suggizon that were cornered, having been set upon by a group of Akkedis. From the makeshift weapons the Akkedis yielded, he assumed they were untrained men, simply fighting to save their city. They improvised with any- thing they could grab, such as axes, shovels, forks and other implements and tools.

Sampson, upon seeing his men overrun, joined in the affray, thrusting his sword deep into the belly of the largest and most aggressive of the Akkedis who was swinging a large axe. Despite the fatal wound caused by Sampson's sword that had completely run through the lizard's body, the strength of the Akkedis continued.

The creature swung its axe with momentum and came at them in a downwards arc. The large Akkedis blew with such a force that when it struck Sampson, it knocked him to the floor. Blood gashed out from the wound he received and the Akkedis raised the axe again, readying to deliver the coup de grâce and finish the Suggizon leader off.

Sampson raised his sword to defend himself, but he knew it would not be enough. Gritting himself for the blow, the Akkedis suddenly stumbled to its knees, the axe dropping harmlessly as it fell face forward onto the ground. Standing behind the fallen Akkedis with his bloodied sword in hand stood Qutaybah, a wry smile on his face.

"Come, my friend," Qutaybah said, reaching forward to help Sampson back to his feet. "The battle is still to be won."

The Suggizon fought on. They battled a whole city of Akkedis, showing no sign of weakness. Yet, the Akkedis would not yield willingly and they fought with real ire. In them was a burning fire that can only come from defending your own home.

The streets were littered with the dead and wounded, both Suggizon and Akkedis. Qutaybah knew that the battle was not going to be easy and final victory would hinge on whether Perseus could kill the Lizard Empress. Facing the rising death toll, he hoped that would be soon.

Lord Parsival led the human contingent of the attack forces and had entered the city at the Northern side, close to where the royal structure was situated. His priority was to release the Queen and her party. He was also instructed to help Persues, if necessary, in killing the Lizard Empress. Qutaybah had inferred that this was paramount to the success of this war. With the Akkedis Empress dead, the Lizard army would capitulate, of this he was certain.

As Parsival surveyed the huge numbers of Akkedis laid out before them and ready to defend their city, he hoped Qutaybah was correct, otherwise this day might not end as they had hoped.

Myriam waited patiently for Arriba to return. Fleetingly she worried that they may have been betrayed, but she reassured herself with the knowledge that if it had not been for Arriba, they would probably have been captured once again. Not all Akkedis must be bad, of this she was sure. Maybe, after this was all over, they could restart diplomatic relations with the new Akkedis ruler.

The hiding place that Arriba had taken them to was indeed dry, but it still smelt damp and dank. Whilst sconces lit the walls, they gave off little light, barely illuminating the dark corners of the room.

Stacked around the room were a number of boxes. Curious to what they might hold, Myriam wandered over to them to investigate. Arriba had told them that this was a library, and they were hidden a store room. Perhaps the boxes contained books? Approaching a stack of boxes, she heard a scuffling noise. Assuming it to be some rodent or other critter, she ignored it. Rats had never bothered her. Opening one of the boxes she peered in, seeing that it was indeed full of books.

The Duchess saw Myriam's face light up with a huge smile.

"What have you discovered there?" she called out to her.

"Books, grandmother, some of them written in our language. It seems the Akkedis are not just treacherous and ignorant."

The Duchess approached her granddaughter, intrigued with Myriam's find, as books were always a passion of hers. Suddenly a number of boxes were pushed to one side and a shadowy figure emerged from behind them.

Grabbing the Duchess around the throat, the figure pinned her body close to its own. Scared and panicked eyes stared out from a nervous face as the attacker scanned the people in the room. Myriam gasped as she recognized the one holding her grandmother.

"Ghaffar! I wondered where you had got yourself to."

CHAPTER 46

Ghaffar was feeling pretty pleased with himself. The situation had looked hopeless. The human Queen's protector was free, as was that cursed snake Perseus. He knew that if they caught him there would be no mercy. Hiding until an opportunity to escape presented itself to him seemed the best plan. When he heard female human voices, he could not believe his luck.

"At last, I have found a use for you both other than draining your blood," he said to them, menace in his tone. "I will allow you to sit on that box, Duchess, but I will be right behind you with a very sharp dagger, so I would not advise you to make any wrong moves as you will be first to go."

The Duchess did as she was instructed and sure enough, she could feel the cold body of a lizard man pressing on her back. This particular lizard man she hated very much. He had been the cause of all her recent troubles.

"Ghaffar, should you not be protecting your Empress?" she asked of him.

"You know only too well, if I go to my Empress then I shall only meet my death. I can hear what is happening on the streets. We are under attack, and no doubt from stinking humans. You are a wretched species, untrustworthy and dishonorable," he spat at her.

"Strange, those were my thoughts exactly," the Duchess replied, very calmly, "whenever I thought of you, Ghaffar. You betray your people by not helping to save of your Empress, surely?"

"I have been loyal, securing her the supply of blood that she needed for survival, and where did it get me? Nowhere!" he shouted, his voice echoing around the small chamber. "I should be running all of the mines by now, she promised me that, but no, I had to stay and babysit the human prisoners. Make sure their blood was not stressed, as it did not taste right if it was. Her precious supply. I should not even have been in this city had she stuck to her promises. Empty promises. It has all been for nothing."

"It appears you have much to be angry for, Ghaffar," the Duchess teased him. "I'm surprised you didn't take the opportunity to remove the Empress and rule in her place. Surely you have an army of soldiers?"

"An army of imbeciles more like. Yes, that was my plan, to become her confidante, her right hand man, eventually, with me making all the decisions as she slipped into her dotage. But now, you have ruined all of that, you and your kind, savages. Still, perhaps I have a use for you yet. As my hostage you will take me from this city and to freedom."

"Is that not my dagger?" Myriam shouted out as she recognized Harkan, the knife that contained the stones of Berghein, the source of her family's magic powers. "You wear my ring too, you greedy little reptile. I will have them all returned, immediately," she demanded, knowing full well that Ghaffar would not comply.

"Sorry, Queen Myriam, these gems are my ticket out of here," he told her with great satisfaction. "But I promise you this, this dagger will be the death of your grandmother if you don't do as I tell you. When Arriba returns, I will begin my plan to flee this place, so wait patiently and you will not be harmed. Not yet, anyway."

It seemed a long wait for Arriba. Myriam was beginning to think she would not return, maybe she had been captured by the invading army or even worse, was dead. It was some relief when the door opened and Arriba entered, carrying a bag full of food and blankets. She dropped her bag onto the floor at the sight of Ghaffar, and gasped.

"Come in, Arriba," Ghaffar demanded. "I have errands that you shall run for me. I am rescuing the human Queen and the Duchess, is that not kind of me?"

Arriba knew this not to be true. Ghaffar would do nothing that did not directly benefit him. She would go along with it so she could stay close to the female humans.

"Before I came in here," he said, "I overheard the humans instructing their soldiers not to kill the women and children. They always were a sentimental race," Ghaffar sniggered. "I want you to go find me a female Akkedis outfit. We will be a party of women, running through the streets. The Duchess and her granddaughter will wear cloaks, to disguise themselves. Now go, Arriba, come back with a female tunic and cloaks, quickly."

Arriba rushed out. She did not wish to leave the humans on their own with Ghaffar for too long. She had learned his true nature as he had witnessed him torturing Ganry with those dreadful insects. He was not to be trusted in any way and she must find a way to save the human Queen and Duchess.

CHAPTER 47

Ganry let Perseus lead their small group. He knew this part of the Akkedis Empress' chambers better than he did, having explored it as a snake when they were supposedly kept in chains.

Perseus briefed them on all that was happening. The city was under attack from humans and the Suzzigon, Perseus's kin. He told Linz that a troop of lakemen were also among the attackers, as were soldiers from the kingdom. This cheered everyone, boosting their confidence for the task that lay ahead.

They followed Perseus's lead through the dark passageways of the underground city. They were surprised not to have come across any Akkedis guards, as they'd expected fierce opposition.

"Surely it will not be this deserted all the way to the Empress' chamber?" Ganry queried.

Perseus just shrugged and continued on.

They found the throne room, unaccosted, the same room where Perseus and Ganry had their last battle and where the treachery of Ghaffar had been fully uncovered. It seemed an age ago since that day, when in fact, it had been only been weeks. The chamber was completely empty so they followed the route they had seen the Akkedis Empress take the last time they were here. It led directly to a set of large double doors.

Empress Gishja, ruler of the Lizard lands had feared the worse. All her guards had deserted her. Personal servants had left too, and she was alone and at the mercies of whatever vile creatures invaded her city. When this was all over, her people would pay a very high price for their cowardice.

She was not sure as to what was happening. Ghaffar had not been to her all day. Normally he came to update her on the state of affairs in her city and the mines. She had become intolerably weak these last few months, her great age finally taking its toll, but Ghaffar had promised to restore her health and extend her existence. All she needed to do was drink the blood of the D'Anjue family and her strength would slowly be restored.

It had seemed so easy when Ghaffar had brought her the old Duchess. It had worked. D'Anjue blood restored her health, but when the old female could provide no more, her own condition had soon deteriorated. Drinking the blood, it seemed, was a double edged sword. It did work, but when it stopped she rapidly declined. That's when Ghaffar had the idea to lure the rest of the D'Anjue family to the lizard city.

When they had captured the four members of the D'Anjue family, she had blood aplenty and again it restored her, but her body needed more and more every day. Without the thick red juices, her condition quickly worsened, and now she had not had any for two days. Her body was weak and frail. Curse Ghaffar for this. She could have seen out her reign with dignity, or died fighting the invaders. Instead, he had reduced her to a weak, feeble and broken Empress.

She could hear the sounds of battle in the city, but she had no way of knowing who would be the victor. The Akkedis soldiers would fight well to protect their city. She just hoped that it would be enough. Gishja cursed her weak body, confining her to this bed. If she was to die, she wanted to die with her people, fighting the invaders.

She heard someone approach, before the doors burst open. Sensing they were foes, she knew her time had come. There would be no begging for her life. She would die proud, smiling her defiance.

All four of them drew their swords as they pushed open the doors to her chamber. The room seemed completely deserted, no soldiers, no servants, nothing. In the center of the room stood a large bed, and in the dim light of the chamber they could just make out the shape of a prone body. As they drew closer they each recognized the Akkedis Empress. Bereft of her blood supply for the last few days, she had declined quickly. Surrounding her, they realized that she was close to death.

The Empress watched them keenly as they approached. "So, it has come to this, has it?" she said, staring Ganry in the eye. "I am to die at the hands of humans. How humiliating," she laughed.

"No, Akkedis Empress, you are to die at the hands of a Suggizon," Perseus told her.

She looked at him, her courage wavered for just a second. She knew the Suggizon were capable of killing a victim very slowly, by crushing it and swallowing it whole, gradually digesting it. That process could last for days.

"I have no intention of consuming your evil body," he mocked her. "The risk of contamination would be too high."

"This is to be my end then? The end of my glorious reign, at the hands of a filthy Suggizon. Do your worst, I fear you not. You are far beneath me, snake man, and I have no fear of you or your people. You deserved to be extinct. There cannot be many of you left."

"You think wrong, Gishja," Perseus said, smiling. "We are many and we attack your city as we speak. Your soldiers litter the streets with their bodies and soon the mines, and your homes, will be ours. We will take those who survive and treat them as slaves."

Ganry, Linz and Hendon, all raised their swords up above the Empress.

"It is time," Perseus nodded at his companions.

"For my Queen, and the Duchess," Ganry proclaimed.

"For my Uncle, Chief Clay, and all the lakelanders' who's blood you have stolen," Linz added.

Hendon was the last to speak.

"I seek my own personal revenge on you, for the malice you have inflicted on me, though I would not seek it on your people, for they have done me no harm."

With that all three plunged their swords into the chest of the Akkedis Empress. She did not cry out or attempt to protect herself as the blades easily pierced her scaly skin.

She lay there, still alive, breath escaping her mouth in short rasping gasps.

Perseus raised up his sword in two hands, above the Empress' prone body. "For the Suggizon, who you almost killed to extinction."

In one clean stroke, Perseus brought his sword down, the sharp edge cutting across her neck and separating her head from her body.

It was done, all life had left the decrepit body. Empress Gishja's cruel reign was at an end.

CHAPTER 48

At the other side of the city to where Sampson led the Suggizon, the humans, commanded by Lord Parsival, were making progress into the Akkedis defenses. The Akkedis had fought hard but now they were losing ground.

A separate force to Parsival's, the lakemen, were attacking in unison, but these were less disciplined troops and answered to no commander. They were fierce warriors and had a grudge to bear against the Akkedis, built up over years of the Rooggaru feeding from their people and killing their great Chief Clay. They had not yet managed to find their new Chief, Linz, and as far as they were aware, he could already be dead. This made their mood even worse.

They cut through the Akkedis with no mercy, not seeing their victims as living beings, only as the enemy. Kill or be killed was their mantra in this battle. Until they found their chief, they would murder everyone in their path, male, female or child, no questions asked.

They went from home to home, leaving no stone unturned in their frenzy.

Bachov, a Kingdom soldier, had been attached to a Lakeland troop. He would not be party to the slaughter of innocents, and hated the random killing of everything. Killing Akkedis soldiers he had no problem with. A soldier knows of the chances of dying by the sword, but women and children? The lakelanders were killing indiscriminately, even putting young babies to the sword. These actions sickened him.

He kicked open a door to an Akkedis home and quickly scanned the room. It appeared empty. As he was about to leave, he heard a muffled cry from a store cupboard. With his sword extended in front of him, he slowly advanced on the source of the noise.

One hand on the store cupboard door, and his sword raised in his other, he quickly pulled open the door, readying himself to strike. He lowered his sword and his face softened as he saw a female Akkedis with a very young one, cowering in the cupboard.

Bachov put his fingers to his mouth, indicating that they should be quiet. He had no qualms disobeying the order to kill everything living. It came from the lakelanders, so he did not have to follow it. Slowly, he closed the doors, just as a lakeman charged into the room.

"All clear," he said, walking away from the cupboard.

"You lie," the lakeman sneered. "I can see it in your face!" he pushed Bachov to one side and opened the cupboard doors.

"Ha!" he cried as he spotted the Akkedis mother and child, raising his sword ready to strike. "They need to die."

Bachov reacted quickly. He could not watch on as this cruel lakelander slaughtered this woman and child. Bringing the hilt of his sword down onto the back of the attacker's head, he knocked him unconscious.

"I'm not sure if you understand me, but you must stay hidden," Bachov instructed her, before closing the cupboard door.

He grabbed hold of the lakelander under his arms and dragged him out of the home before leaving him in the street. Hopefully when he awoke, he would have no recollection of these events and even if he did, they may both be dead before the day was over.

CHAPTER 49

Ghaffar was pleased his disguise was working well. It fooled both the Akkedis and the attacking forces. He had forced Arriba to lead the group from the front, with him at the rear. If they were to come across anyone, she was to show herself. Whoever stopped them would think they were a simple group of females trying to escape the slaughter. The motivation for Arriba was the fact that she was aware Ghaffar held a knife at the Duchess's back, and one wrong move and she would be dead.

His plan was to make his way to the bridge by the river. This is a good way out of the city, if he could just avoid capture by the Suggizon. He had not decided what to do with the hostages, as much depended on what happened during his escape from the city. It was difficult keeping hold of both the Duchess's arm, and pressing the dagger into her back. Necessary though, for the human Queen would only do as he bid while he threatened the life of her grandmother.

Already he could see the bridge. They did not have far to go now. Having hostages would prove useful and guarantee him safe passage. Once free of the city, he would kill Arriba and the old woman, and use Myriam as ransom to help him set up a new life.

Killing Arriba could prove difficult, as she was a strong, young Akkedis female. In a face to face battle she could probably overcome him, so he would need to be sly when he murdered her. He was puzzled as to why she was helping the humans anyway. Akkedis are taught that self preservation is the only trait to foster. Pity and empathy has no place in an Akkedis's life.

At last they arrived at the bridge, unhindered. This could not have gone any better, and he felt his luck was turning just in time. The ransom for the human Queen would help satisfy his need for funds. His initial intention had been to reach the mines, but it was now far too risky. Instead, the Kingdom would pay a handsome price for the safe return of their monarch.

"On to the bridge, Arriba, do as I say!" he shouted up to her as she began to climb the steps that led there.

They paused at the top of the stairs while Ghaffar scanned the bridge for hostiles. He spotted a group of humans and Suggizon, recognizing two of the men.

"Hendon, Hendon, we're over here!" he heard Myriam's voice shout out.

So over confident in how his escape plan was going, he had been too lapse with her. He struck her hard across the face and she stumbled back, falling onto the ground.

"Keep quiet," he hissed at her, "or I will gut the Duchess, and then you."

He turned to Arriba who was still in the lead, and ordered her to keep moving.

Arriba had also spotted the two human males who had been part of Myriam's party. She was unsure if they had heard Myriam's cry for help and was considering shouting out, when she saw them move towards the bridge. She smiled to herself. Ghaffar hissed at her to get moving, but she refused, standing stock still and awaiting for the arrival of the soldiers.

Hendon was first on the scene. He was puzzled at first. He thought he had heard Myriam shout out, but these were a group of Akkedis females. As he looked at the one on the ground, she pulled back her hood, revealing herself.

"Myriam, is that you?" Hendon said, shocked. "Are you hurt?" he asked, noticing blood trickling from her nose.

He turned to the female who had struck her and instantly recognized that it was Ghaffar, dressed as the opposite gender. Furious with Ghaffar for striking Myriam down, he looked at him fiercely.

"You odious little beast!" he yelled into Ghaffar's face, spittle spraying from his mouth. "Your time has come. You have caused enough trouble for my family name."

Linz looked on in surprise at Hendon's outburst. He had known him some time now, and they had faced many adversities together, but in all that time he had never known Hendon to lose control.

Myriam and the females moved away from Ghaffar, to stand behind Linz and Hendon.

"I challenge you to the death, Ghaffar," Hendon thundered. "Your days on this world are numbered!"

Ghaffar almost chuckled. He had become quite familiar with the humans and this one, of them all, was the weakest and most naive. He would be easy to beat, even in combat.

"Very well, Hendon, but when I kill you, I will be allowed to walk free, yes?" Ghaffar demanded his prize at the onset.

"Do not concern yourself with such matters, Ghaffar," Hendon replied. "You will not walk free from this. I will slay you down, and no one will mourn your passing."

"No, don't let this happen," Myriam cried out. "He will kill you, Hendon. He is far too crafty for your gentle nature."

Hendon put up his palm and held out his arm towards Myriam, indicating that he did not care to listen to her.

"The deal is set," Ghaffar laughed. "To the death it is then, human. Prepare to meet your maker."

CHAPTER 50

Perseus stood on the balcony of the Empress' residence, her gruesome head in his hands as he surveyed the battle below him. The Akkedis were in retreat, but still they had fought fiercely. The streets of the city strewn with corpses and rivers of blood ran in the gutters.

The Akkedis army was beaten, but they had given no ground without fighting. This was their city and they had been determined to fight until the very last one of them was left standing. They owed it to their families, they owed it to their Empress.

Perseus had asked Ganry to climb up to the bell tower that rose above the royal residence, and on his signal to sound the bells. As they peeled out across the city, everyone paused and looked up. Perseus held out the head of the Akkedis Empress before him, her sightless eyes staring over her subjects.

"Enough!" he cried out at the top of his voice. "Empress Gishja is dead. The battle is lost. Lay down your arms and you will be spared."

With that he threw her head down onto the street below. It hit the ground with a thud and bounced once, before rolling to the feet of the Akkedis soldiers.

"All is lost," the leader of the group wailed. "Our Empress is dead!"

A murmur rose from the Akkedis soldiers as they stared at the head of their dead ruler. For a moment, Perseus was uncertain if his plan had worked. It seemed that the Akkedis soldiers would keep on fighting. But eventually, one by one, they threw down their arms and retreated from the battle. Soon, word had spread to other Akkedis soldiers in other parts of the city, and they too surrendered.

The battle was over. A heavy price had been paid by both sides, but the city was now in Suggizon hands.

The defeated army were massed in groups and kept in open spaces, guarded by a few soldiers. Now the Empress was dead, the Akkedis showed no signs of retaliation.

Few Akkedis would mourn the death of Gishja. She had lived for over three hundred years, and two hundred of those as Empress. After murdering her father, she ruled with an iron fist. Some thought her a cruel leader, hard on her people, but they had thrived under her leadership. The gem mines had been in full productivity and the wealth they brought had made the underground city as beautiful as any in the world.

Still, for most Akkedis it was a hard life, working the mines. Even the children, once old enough, would be made to dig for gems. For those who did not work the mines, every other Akkedis had a job to do, daily tasks to perform for the running of the city.

Now the Akkedis had no Empress, they had no leader. Their army, although brave and fearless, were poorly trained. Gishja never cared for such things, believing they were safe from attack in their underground city. She had the army doubling up as guards at the mines, so most of the time they were out of the city. A poor judgment on this day, her last. Now her people were cowed and beaten, and feared for their own future.

Perseus and the Suggizons had gained much from the Empress' death, and the defeat of the Akkedis.

Qutaybah, who had financed this expedition, had made a great return on his investment now that the gem mines were in his control. Another of his motivations was to see the Suggizon, a race he greatly admired, in a permanent home at last. Qutaybah felt this was only fair and just, as it had been Empress Gishja who had overseen the almost complete annihilation of the Suggizon race. Whilst he did feel some sympathy for the Akkedis, he believed they would be well cared for, even as slaves.

Sampson stood at a distance as he watched a human on the bridge confronting what looked like a group of Akkedis females. He could not ignore the situation. He had heard how some of the humans were slaughtering the woman and children, so he had to act. He headed towards the bridge to intervene, but something tugged at his senses and caused him to pause. He sensed something he had not felt for a while. He could feel the presence of his brother.

A strong pat on his back nearly knocked him over and he quickly spun around to confront his attacker.

"Now then, dear brother, if I had been an Akkedis, you would be dead," Perseus chided him.

"Perseus!" he yelled with elation, even among all this death and destruction there was joy to be felt.

They embraced, happy to hold the other in their arms.

"It has been too long, Perseus," Sampson said as he pulled away, reluctantly. It had been years since he had seen his younger sibling.

"You have grown," he said to his little brother.

"And you, have shrunk, I'm sure," Perseus joked back.

"Well, that's what comes of being a parent to three." Sampson was keen to share the good news of his family.

"I'm an uncle to three? Sampson, you have been busy procreating, I see."

Sampson noticed that Perseus was looking over at the events on the bridge.

"You know him?" he asked.

"I do, and we should not interfere. The humans have their own reasons for this battle, just as we do." Perseus wondered at what Hendon was up to. He was the more reserved of the group and was the last one he expected to see confronting Ghaffar.

"You know I cannot allow this human to kill an Akkedis female in front of our people," Sampson tried to explain. "We need to learn compassion."

"That is not a female that he confronts. It is a cowardly Akkedis male, Ghaffar, who has been the cause of many troubles for the humans. The others with him on the bridge, are the human Queen Myriam and the Duchess D'Anjue. Whilst it seems out of character for Hendon to behave in this manner, there must be reasoning behind his actions. Please leave this to me, brother. The events may seem strange to you, but all shall be resolved in the end."

His brother nodded in agreement and Perseus headed for Linz, who had not gone on to the bridge.

"Perseus, we got lost and found ourselves with your people instead of mine," Linz said as he spotted the shape-shifters arrival.

"Why does Hendon put himself in danger?" Perseus asked the young chief, knowing it would normally be Linz who did the fighting.

"Hendon heard Myriam call out his name, and he saw Ghaffar strike her down. He told me, in no uncertain terms, that I was to stand down. I believe he has one of his tricks to play out."

"Tricks?" Perseus was confused, he knew nothing of such things.

"He's up to something, but I'm not sure what it is. I think he wants to play his part in this war and rid the world of Ghaffar. I'll only interfere if he does something stupid," Linz said, making no effort to go to the bridge.

"As will I," Perseus agreed, even though all his instincts urged him to go and assist the human Queen and Duchess as he had promised Qutaybah.

Yet, something about Hendon, who stood on that bridge, told his senses that there was more to him than meets the eye. Despite his weakened appearance, he needed no assistance. He would watch and wait, as Linz had suggested, and only interfere if needed.

CHAPTER 51

When Ganry found Parsival, they had just finished rounding up the surrendered Akkedis in that part of the city. He was also in a fierce argument with a lakelander.

"No more. I will not let you slaughter surrendered troops, do you understand?" Parsival was almost shouting at the lakelander.

The lakeman reluctantly shrugged his agreement, ordering his men to stand down.

"We will do as you ask for now, Lord Parsival, but mark my words, if Chief Linz has died at their hands, we will not leave a single Akkedis alive in this city."

Ganry approached the lakeman speaker. "Your Chief lives my friend, or at least he did a few hours ago. I last saw him with Hendon, the forest dweller."

Ganry's words brought great rejoicing from the lakelanders. They set off in search of their missing chief.

"You give them good news, Ganry," the young Lord said, relieved. "It has been difficult trying to contain their bloodlust. They are fierce fighters and spare no-one, not even the women and children."

"I left Myriam with a female Akkedis. She will be heartbroken if anything happens to her Akkedis friends," Ganry said, more to himself than aloud.

"You have news on Queen Myriam and the Duchess too, are they safe?" Parsival asked, hopeful.

"They were, Lord Parsival, but I've not seen her for a few hours. She was hidden by an Akkedis female, but I don't know where," Ganry explained.

The underground streets were deathly quiet, now that the fighting was finished.

"Who's leading the armies?" Ganry asked.

Parsival advised Ganry on the chain of command for the attack. "Qutaybah and his mercenaries have been fighting together with the Suggizon leader, Sampson. I have been leading the Kingdom men, but the lake-landers are a force unto themselves and take no orders from anyone."

"Can you lead me to Qutaybah? I must see if Queen Myriam is with him."

Parsival nodded agreement and with a few chosen men, he escorted Ganry through the streets of the city. The dead Akkedis still lay where they had fallen, covered in fallen dust and sand.

"They will need to start clearing the dead soon. Disease will spread like wild fire down here," Ganry said to Parsival as he followed him through the mess. "We need to gather our troops and get out of here."

"I could not agree more," the Lord replied, turning around to nod his head. "As soon as we get to the Suggizon, I'll find Qutaybah and inform him that we're retrieving our own troops. The sooner we are out of here the better. Humans are not meant to live underground, it is too stifling and constricting. Give me the open air and the wide fields of the Kingdom, any day."

They continued their journey in silence, maybe from respect of the scattered dead, or simply from exhaustion. As they entered a new area of the city, Parsival spotted one of the Suggizon soldiers.

The Lord stopped Ganry where he stood, and approached the Suggizon soldier himself to find out where his leader was situated. Armed with the information, he called over to Ganry and they continued in their trek. They did not have far to go and soon came upon a whole group of Suggizon clustered in a crowd. It seemed they were stood watching something. Ganry and Parsival made their way through them, grateful that at least the fighting was over in this part of the city as well.

It was soon obvious what was drawing in the crowd. Ganry looked over at a bridge and spotted Hendon, confronting what looked like Ghaffar. His protective nature willed him to rush over to the young man's assistance, especially when he spotted Myriam and the Duchess at the other side of Ghaffar. Perseus appeared by his side, and stopped him.

"This is Hendon's call, leave him to it, Ganry, or at least give him a chance," he pleaded.

Ganry was unsure at first, but then he saw Linz, who was also only observing.

"What is that light that comes from Hendon's staff?" Ganry asked.

"We don't know yet, it happened only seconds ago," Perseus shrugged. "I suspect Hendon is about to show us, so hold tight, for a short while anyway."

CHAPTER 52

Ghaffar circled Hendon with Harkan, Myriam's dagger, held out in front of him. He thought the idiot boy only to be armed with a staff, and this was going to be easier than he thought. Ghaffar was confident that he could easily kill this young fool and be free of the city. He thrust his dagger towards Hendon, not really attempting to stab him, more to let him know that he meant business.

He noted that a crowd was drawing close, and many had come to see what was happening. This made Ghaffar nervous. A deal had been made and freedom promised, but if the mob was to rule, who knew what might happen. Promises could easily be broken. Enough of this fooling around. Ghaffar decided now was the time to end this charade. With the dagger firmly gripped in his hand, he advanced on his opponent.

***

Hendon was not really sure why he had challenged Ghaffar to a duel. Something inside his head had urged him to do so. Now that they were facing each other off, he was beginning to think this was a mistake. He was no fighter, he was a man of words, a man of reasoning.

As Ghaffar circled him, Hendon kept a close eye on his opponent. The Akkedis made a few half hearted attempts to thrust the dagger in Hendon's general direction, but he had so far easily avoided all his efforts. Now, Hendon saw a different look to Ghaffar's features, a hard glint in his eye. This was it. He could see Ghaffar readying himself to strike, and Hendon had no idea what he was going to do.

Suddenly, the staff began to vibrate in Hendon's hand and a bright light burst from the tip of the shaft.

The beam grew bigger and before everybody's eyes, an image of a man appeared in the haze of light, a man dressed in long blue robes and carrying a staff of his own. Hendon, Myriam, Ganry and Linz instantly recognized it as Barnaby.

"Ahh, Ghaffar, we meet at last," the image spoke. "Shame this will be the first and the last time."

Barnaby pointed his own staff at Ghaffar and a bolt of blue lightening shot from the end, striking the Akkedis in the chest. The long blue glowing bolt flowed into Ghaffar, shaking him violently as the current coursed through his body. The convulsing body began to smoke, and a few seconds later, it burst into flames. Screaming in agony as he fell to the floor, the fire consumed him. Within moments, Ghaffar fell still and silent.

The Akkedis traitor was dead.

"There," Barnaby said, turning to Hendon, "that should do it, that one always does the trick."

"Is he dead?" Hendon asked.

"Oh yes, Ghaffar is no more," Barnaby replied. "I must be off now. And so must you," Barnaby turned to Myriam. "Your Kingdom needs you, Myriam, and you too, Duchess."

"Barnaby, you have helped us so much," Myriam replied, still puzzled at the events. "I'm glad to have the opportunity to thank you in person," she finished, as she walked towards him. "Can you not stay and help us rebuild the Kingdom?"

"No, my time here is done now, but I will pass on much that I know to my apprentice, Hendon," he smiled, looking over at the forest dweller.

Barnaby's image began to fade and flicker, as though he were a reflection on water.

"Now then, where's Ganry?" Barnaby asked, scanning the crowd of people gathered.

Ganry heard his name and came forward, heading towards the bridge.

"I'm here, old man!" he shouted over.

"Ah, just want to tell you that you are quite right. There is no such thing as magic, not if you don't believe it!" Barnaby said, as if that should explain everything. "Oh dear," he exclaimed. "It seems I'm fading fast."

Barnaby's image wavered before their eyes and had almost faded from view.

"Oh, one last thing, Hendon."

Hendon turned, wondering what pearls of wisdom Barnaby had for him before he left.

"On your way back through the desert there is an oasis. There you will find a coconut tree I planted many years ago. It's perfect for the hot and thirsty traveler, providing shade and refreshment. Please, don't forget to visit it, and talk to it nicely. I do worry it will get rather lonely. I wish I'd planted two now… Hmm now there's an idea. I'll send you some seeds, look under your pillow tonight, my boy."

With those strange words, his image began to fade, and soon he was gone.

CHAPTER 53

Perseus led the the group through the dark tunnels to the outside world.

"I asked Perseus to show us the quickest way out," Ganry explained to the party as they neared the exit. "At the moment the city isn't safe. There are still a few pockets of resistance fighting, and with the risk of disease and the possibility of walls collapsing around us, I felt we'd be better out here."

At last Ganry spotted light up ahead. The way out was only a few yards in front of them. They all quickened their pace, after so long below ground, they were eager to breathe fresh air and see the sunshine once again.

Ganry was the first to step into the bright sunlight and breathe deeply. No one spoke, they simply enjoyed the cool breeze on their faces. Although the desert was a hot place to be, after the stifling heat down in the city, the air up here felt fresh and breathable.

"Oh, Ganry, it was worth coming out just to feel the air on our skin," Myriam laughed, opening up her arms wide as if to embrace the very elements. "This is glorious. I never thought we would see the sky or the sun ever again. Thank you, Perseus. We will never be able to repay our gratitude to you."

The Duchess was the last out of the cave, supported by Arriba. She was still weak after her trial of the last few months, but she was determined to see her homeland once again. She leaned on Arriba, who had stayed with her, nursing her to health. The Duchess thought she probably felt guilty at what her people had done to them, not that any blamed her personally, even though she was the one that bled them to feed her Empress.

The immediate area following the tunnel was banked by high stone walls and natural rocks that hid the main entrance of the city. A city that was now to be rebuilt for a different race.

They decided to make camp here. It was close to the tunnels and they wanted to be nearby for when the rest of the human armies came out. Arriba made a makeshift den for the human Queen and Duchess, and they laid down in the shade. The pure luxury of fresh air to breath was intoxicating. They lay on their capes, in Arriba's den, and soaked up the feeling of being once again free and out in the open.

They didn't have long to wait before the invading forces started to emerge from the tunnel. Linz led his own tribe, the lake people, with Hendon by his side. Lord Parsival led the Kingdom army with Qutaybah and his men just behind. Soon tents were erected and fires burned, as the forces settled down for the night, preparing for the long journey home across the Saraba desert.

"My dear," the Duchess asked of Arriba, "will you go to Qutaybah and lead him to me? I would go myself but I fear my legs would not carry me."

"Of course, Duchess, I will help you in any way I can," Arriba replied, honestly. "You must rest and I will bring him to you."

Arriba set off through the camp in search. The camps had a large number of wounded soldiers, clearly the battle had been a bloody one. She wondered how many of her own had survived. The human soldiers gave her a cold stare as she made her way through, especially the lakelanders, some of whom jeered and spat at her as she passed them by. She was beginning to fear for her safety when Ganry was suddenly by her side, taking her by the arm.

"It's not safe for you here, Arriba. Not everyone knows that you have helped the Queen and Duchess escape."

"I am on an errand for the Duchess. She wishes for Qutaybah to call on her," she nervously explained.

"Let me escort you then," he suggested, and she was quietly relieved.

Soon they were in the right camp and speaking to Qutaybah. He returned immediately with Arriba.

As they entered the shelter where the Duchess was resting, she started to rise.

"No, no, Duchess," Qutaybah said, rushing to her side and sitting down next to her in the shaded sands. "You have been through too much already," he said, taking her delicate hands into his large, strong ones.

"We have many camels, and you will ride in comfort from hereon. It's important that you recover to be the strong woman I know."

"Oh, you flatter me, desert man," she laughed back at him, a clear fondness in her face.

Qutaybah stayed a while to chat with the Duchess. They had much to talk about and their discussion went on long into the night.

"Rest now, my Lady," Qutaybah finally said. "Tomorrow we travel across the desert, and you will need all your strength for that."

Qutaybah left the Duchess to rest and began organizing the caravan for tomorrow's trek across the Saraba. Keen to get home and sleep in a real bed, he was getting too old for these adventures, he told himself.

Arriba slept little that night. She sat by the camp fire and watched the lakelanders with a seething hatred in her heart. She especially watched every move that Linz made.

She had not realized whilst he was imprisoned in the rooms that he was a lakelander, and the leader no less. She knew it was these people who had killed many female Akkedis and children. They were all murdered in cold blood while they cowered in fear.

She realized now that the lakemen were the true monsters. A blood price must be paid, and vengeance exacted. She would do this final task for her people. The lakeland leader still lived. But he would not for long. She closed her eyes and planned to mete out justice.

CHAPTER 54

With the underground city secured enough for the Suggizon to begin their work, it was time for the humans to leave. Those Akkedis who had survived were given a choice, either banishment in the far reaches of the desert, or slavery. Most chose the desert, but some remained to be servants of the Suggizon.

Arriba had agreed to join the Duchess's party. She would go to the Kingdom and live her life in a human castle, serving the royal family. Myriam was a little reluctant, though Arriba had more than proven her worth. She was an Akkedis and surely would still have loyalties to that race, but her grandmother had become fond of her. With Duchess D'Anjue still weakened, Myriam had relented and hoped that Arriba could be happy away from her own people.

The caravan set off in the late hours of the afternoon when the sun was going down. Qutaybah was in in the lead, followed by the lakemen and Chief Linz, and then the Kingdom soldiers with their Queen and Duchess. It had grown in size as they had all joined together. There would be plenty of stop off points to gain more supplies, so Qutaybah did not worry over small details.

Myriam was pleased to learn from Ganry that the Suggizon, and Perseus, would remain in the employ of Qutaybah. He had been offered freedom to help his people and stay with his brother to build up their new city, but he declined. His heart was with his master, Qutaybah, who had done much for him and his race. He promised his brother he would visit frequently, if only to keep an eye on him.

The journey progressed well, the sun was setting and the night ushered in a welcome coolness. Myriam could see little through the curtained window of her small box that perched between the humps of a camel. She thought it a strange contraption and would have preferred to have traveled by simply riding a saddle, the way she had journeyed here.

Qutaybah had insisted on the Queen and Duchess traveling in some comfort. He told them it befitted their status. Myriam had to agree that these travel arrangements would suit her grandmother as she was still too weak to travel by saddle.

They stopped as the sun began to rise and cast its yellow glow over the desert sands. It was the oasis that Barnaby had mentioned, the one with the coconut tree. It seemed to have an abundance of fruit and the whole party enjoyed the milk and sweet flesh. As Myriam wandered around she came across Hendon. He had dug a little hole close to the coconut tree and was putting something in the ground.

Hendon, hearing her approach, turned to greet her.

"I awoke this morning with a small pouch on my pillow, and lo and behold inside were these seeds," he smiled, remembering his discovery. "Barnaby's doing, of that I am certain. So here I am planting a seed by this tree, so one day, it will have a companion, just as Barnaby wished. It is my intention to plant seeds, two at a time so they don't get lonely, at every oasis we stop at on our journey."

"You'll be glad to be back in your forest, instead of these dry lands, won't you?" she asked, knowing the answer without hearing it. Hendon only smiled his agreement. Myriam continued, "I too will be glad to leave these lands and return to the castle. I miss my home and I've not had chance to settle in since I lost my mother and father. I still haven't officially mourned their passing, so I intend on setting aside some time for the city to mourn them too."

"Time goes by quickly," another voice chimed, as Chief Linz approached his dear friends. "We passed those rocks not so far back where we were attacked by the sand worms, and I lost my mentor, Wyatt. I too intend on taking time for mourning. He was a good, brave man."

"That he was, Linz," Myriam agreed. "We have had no time to reflect on our losses. It seems we staggered from one disaster to another. Now, hopefully, we can grow old in peace."

"I'm glad to see the Duchess so happy," Ganry said as he joined their conversation. "She is growing stronger every day."

Myriam smiled at Ganry as he approached the small group.

"What are you all doing among these trees?" Ganry asked. "The night draws in fast, you don't need to be in the shade."

"We're watching the growth of the magic coconut tree," Hendon replied.

"Ah, now there you go again," Ganry gestured with his arms in the air. "You heard Barnaby, he said there is no real magic, it's all in your head… or whatever it was he said."

"I don't believe that to be true, Ganry," Myriam said. "Otherwise how can Hendon talk to the animals, that is magic if ever I saw it?"

"Perhaps," was all Ganry would commit to.

"Dinner is served," Arriba called over to them.

"Wonderful, I'm starving," Linz replied. "I'm a growing young man and I have a lot of meat to put back on my bones," he said, as they all laughed heartily at him.

There was a happy and relaxed atmosphere at dinner. Qutaybah and the Duchess joined them, providing the refreshment of a keg of ale.

Arriba served the meals to each and every one of them, paying particular attention to Linz's dish.

ABOUT THE AUTHOR

Jon Kiln writes heroic fantasy.

Sign up to his mailing list or contact him at
www.JonKiln.com

More Books by Jon Kiln

Blade Asunder Series
Mercenary
Guardian
Warden

Honor Bound Series
Forsaken
Betrayal

Veiled Dagger Series
Assassin's Quest

Printed in Great Britain
by Amazon.co.uk, Ltd.,
Marston Gate.